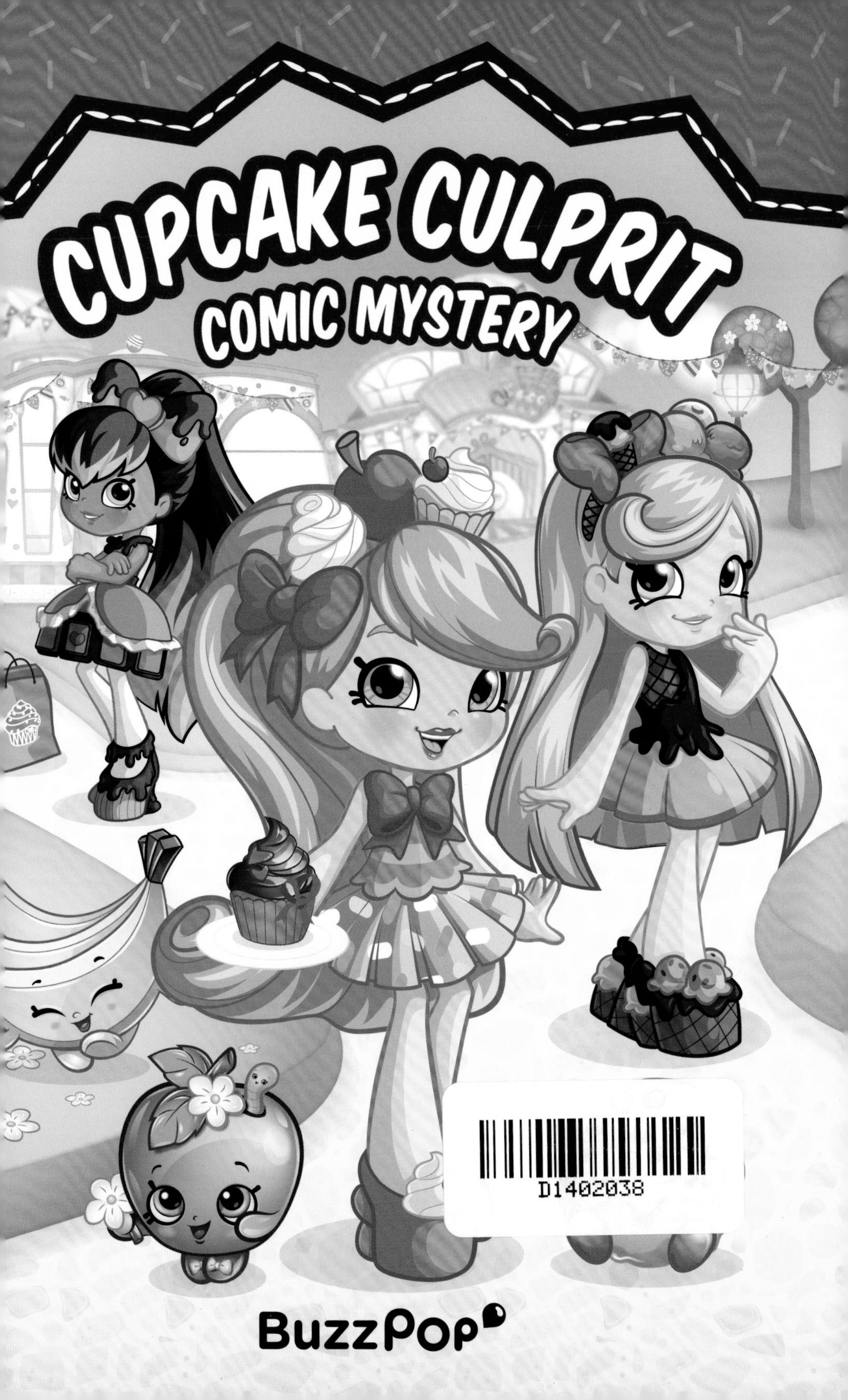
CUPCAKE CULPRIT
COMIC MYSTERY
BuzzPop

BuzzPop

An imprint of Bonnier Publishing USA
251 Park Avenue South, New York, NY 10010

Manufactured in CHINA HOX 0618
First Edition 1 3 5 7 9 10 8 6 4 2
ISBN 978-1-4998-0782-0
buzzpopbooks.com
bonnierpublishingusa.com

Under license by:

29 Grange Road, Cheltenham, VIC 3192, Australia
www.moosetoys.com
info@moosetoys.com

RUB THE STICKERS TO RELEASE THE DELICIOUS SCENT!

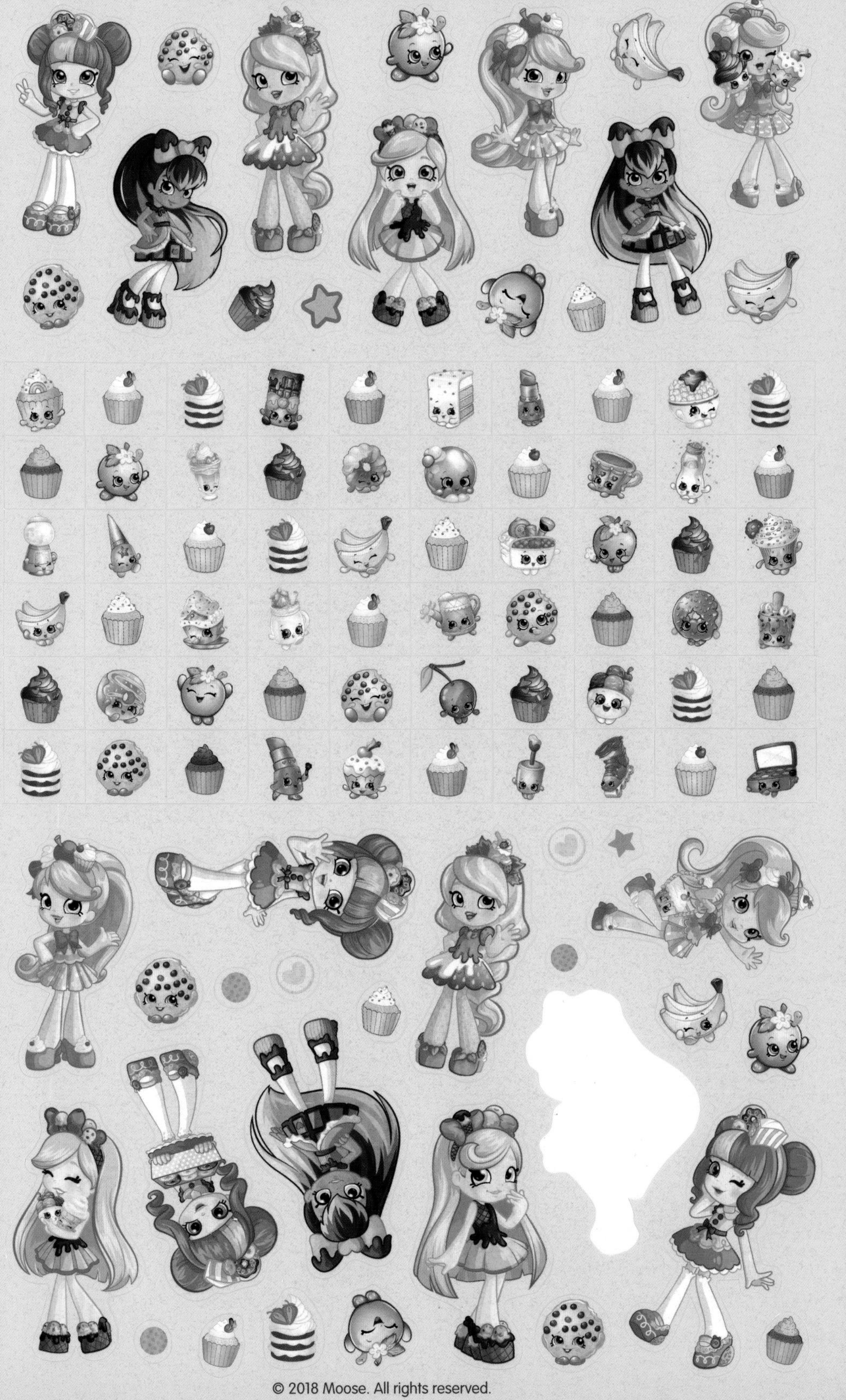

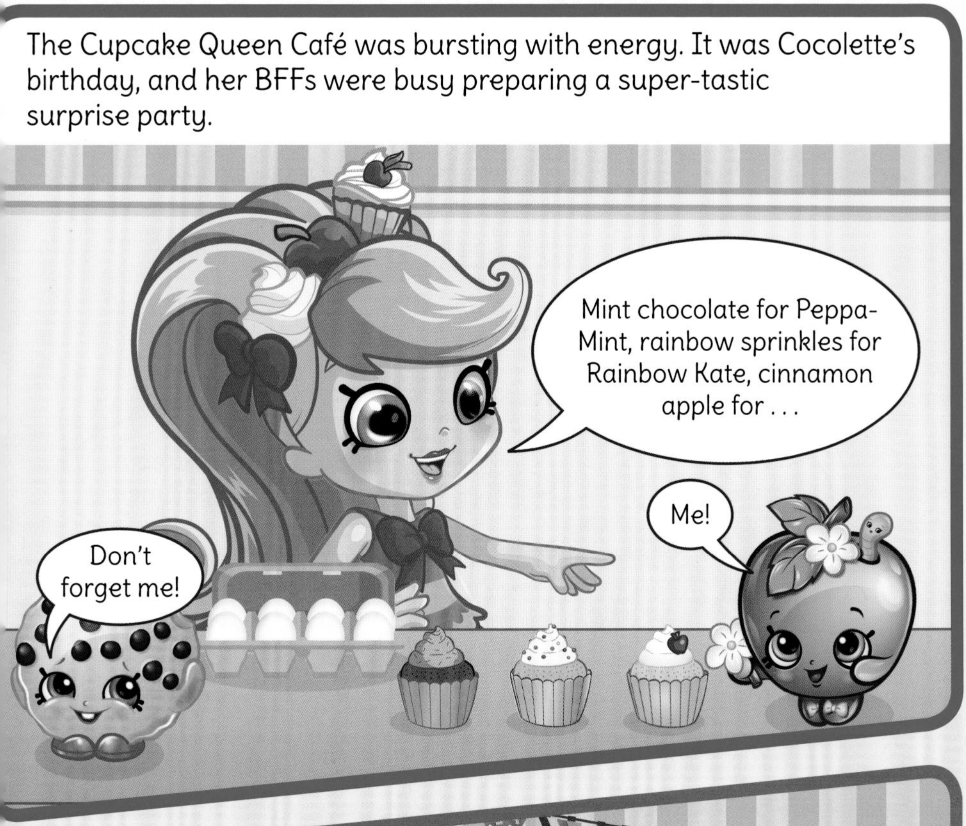
The Cupcake Queen Café was bursting with energy. It was Cocolette's birthday, and her BFFs were busy preparing a super-tastic surprise party.
Mint chocolate for Peppa-Mint, rainbow sprinkles for Rainbow Kate, cinnamon apple for . . .
Me!
Don't forget me!

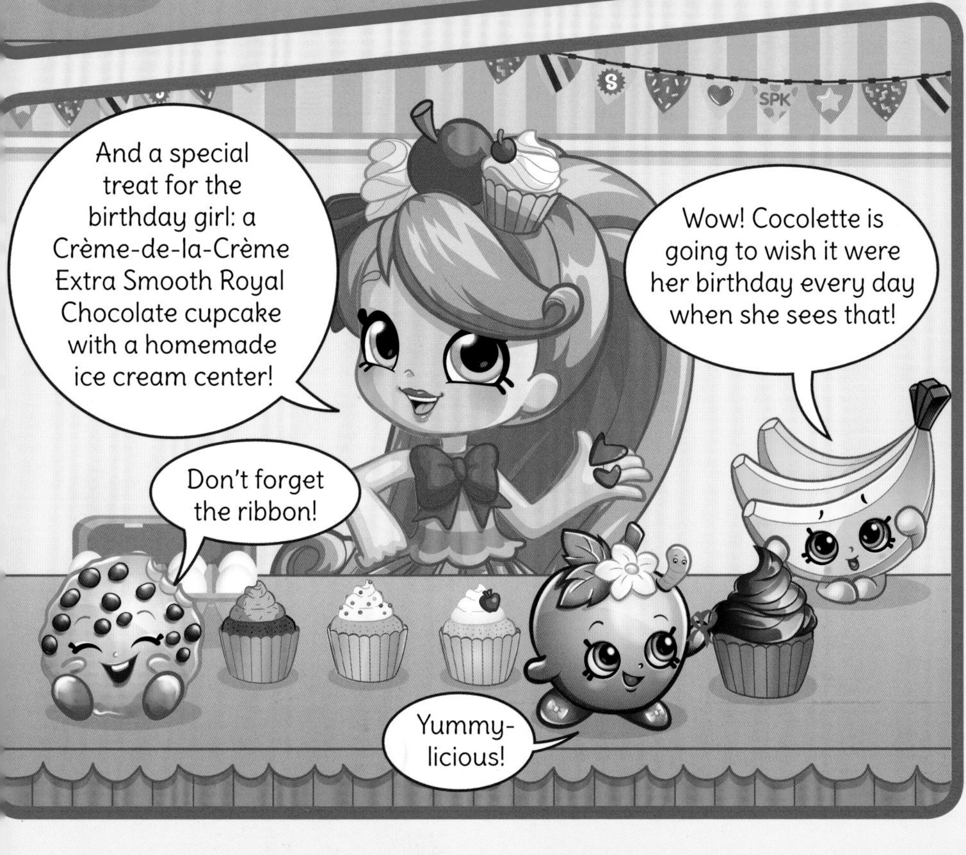
And a special treat for the birthday girl: a Crème-de-la-Crème Extra Smooth Royal Chocolate cupcake with a homemade ice cream center!
Wow! Cocolette is going to wish it were her birthday every day when she sees that!
Don't forget the ribbon!
Yummy-licious!
SPK

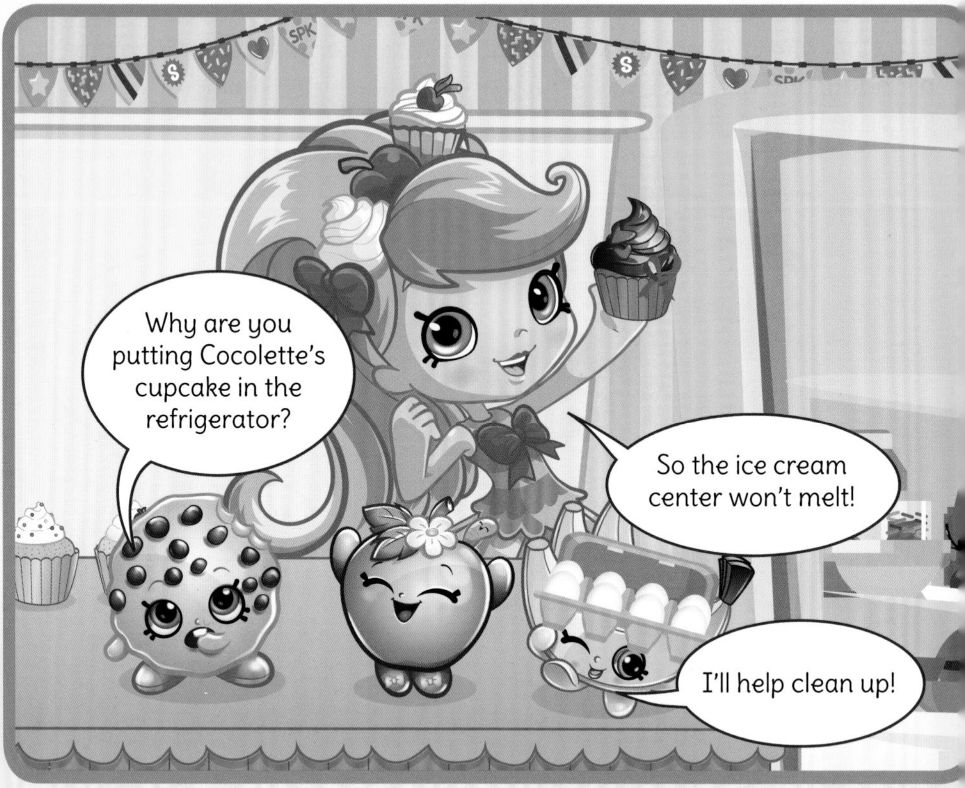
Why are you putting Cocolette's cupcake in the refrigerator?
So the ice cream center won't melt!
I'll help clean up!

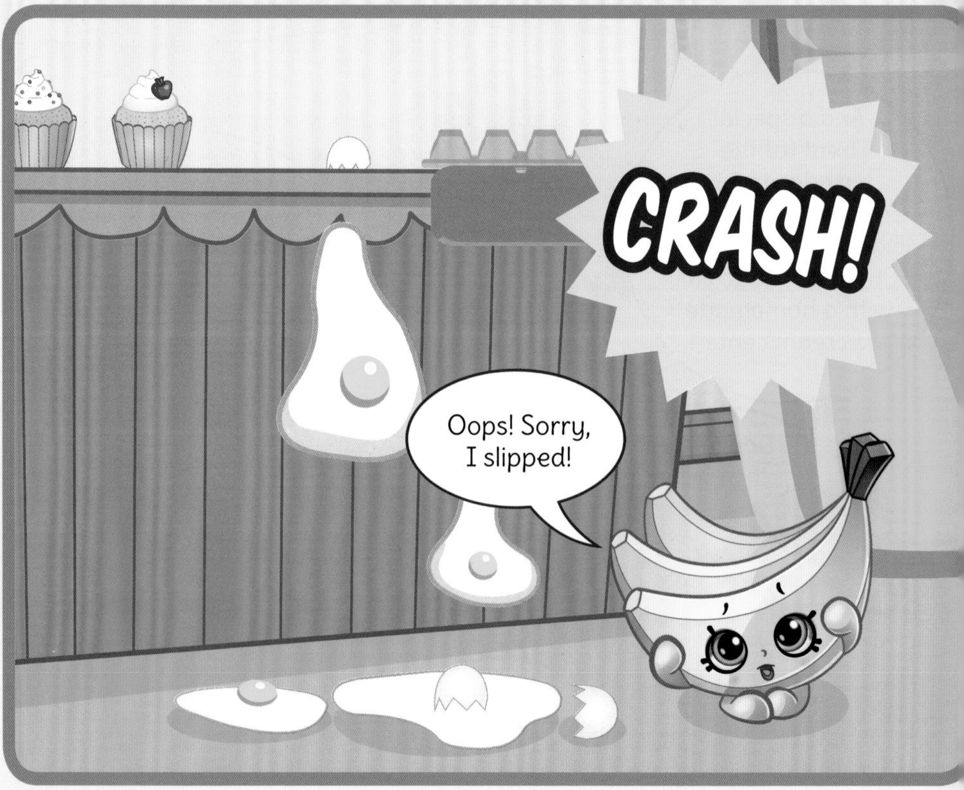
CRASH!
Oops! Sorry, I slipped!

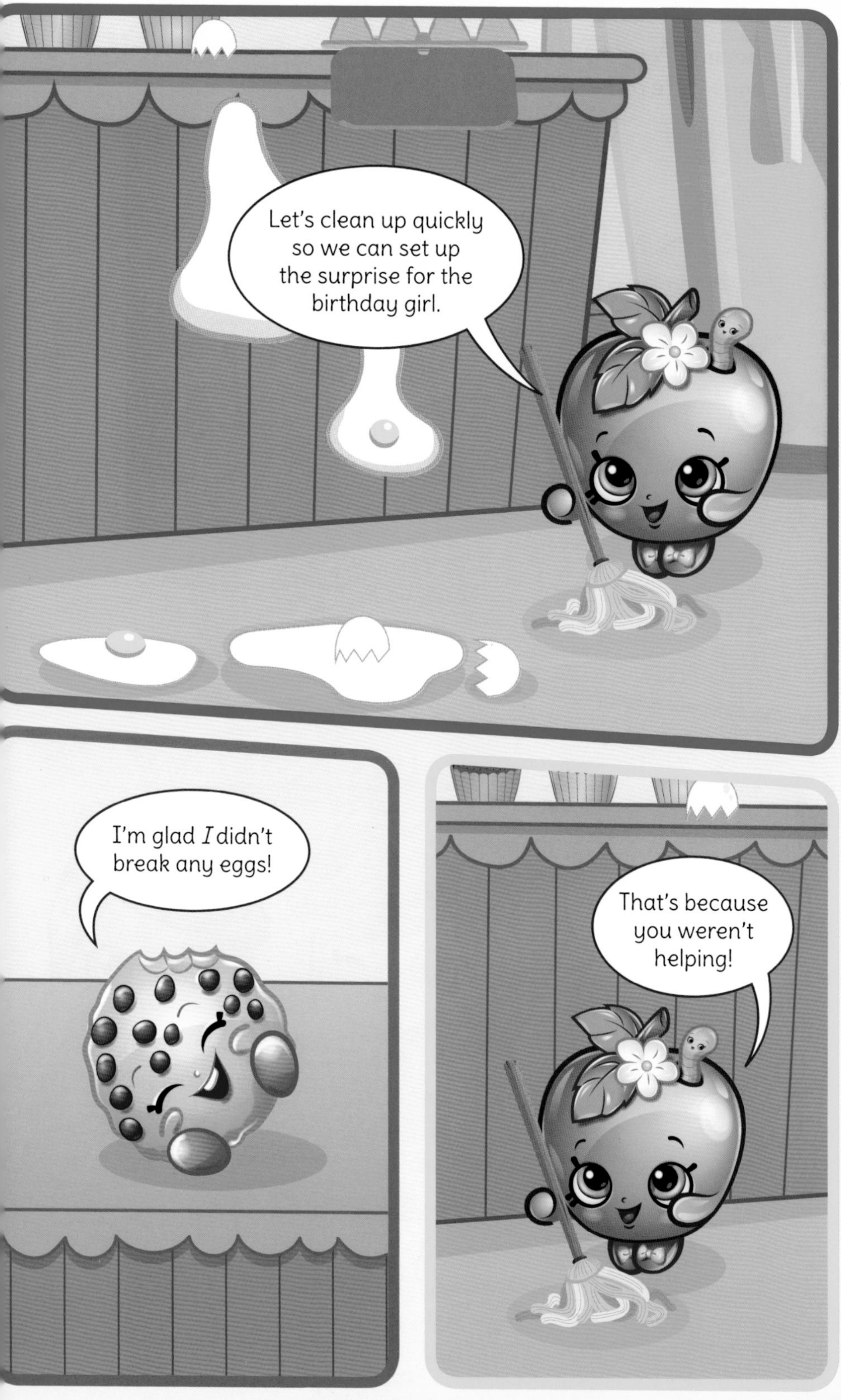
Let's clean up quickly so we can set up the surprise for the birthday girl.
I'm glad *I* didn't break any eggs!
That's because you weren't helping!

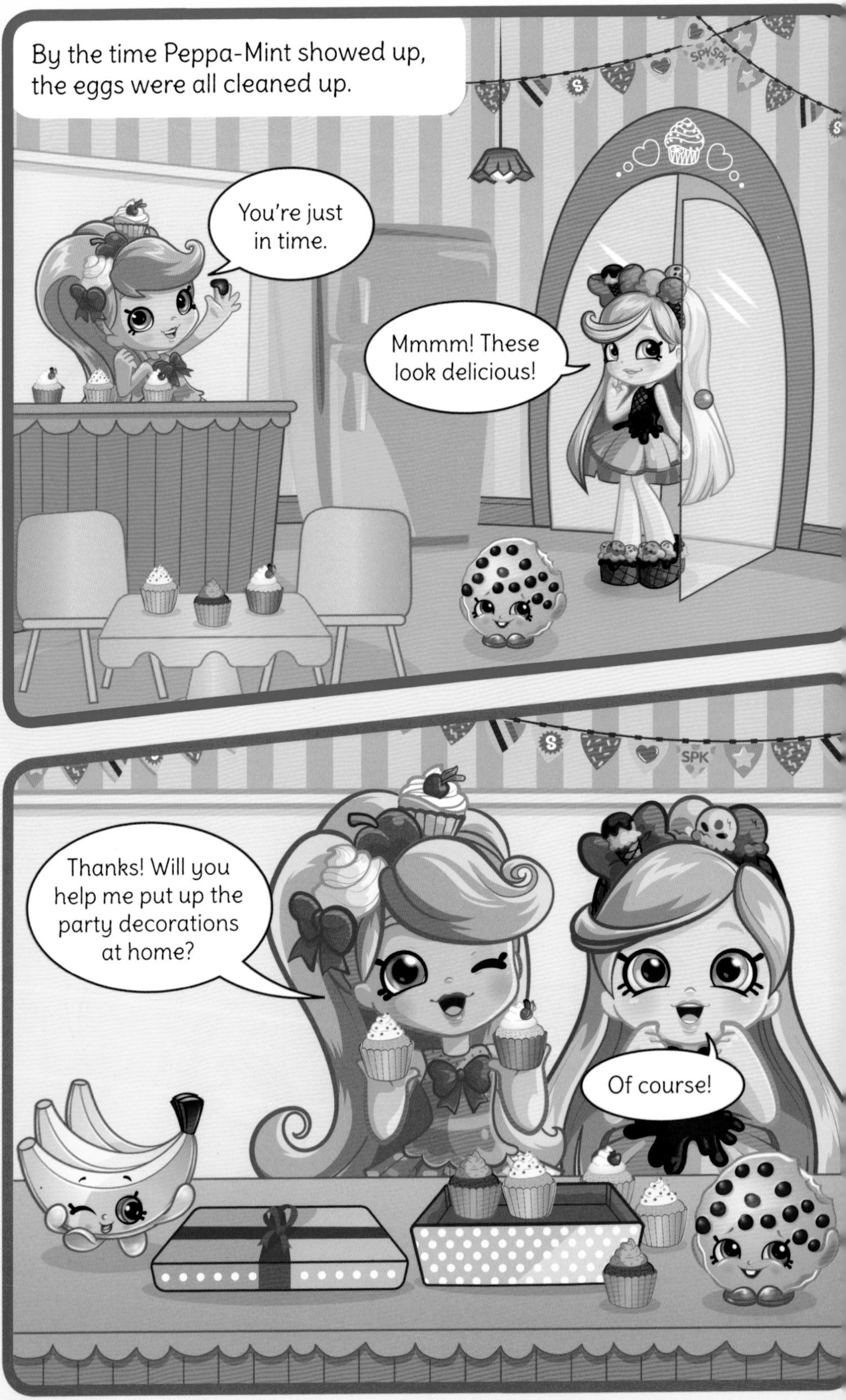
By the time Peppa-Mint showed up, the eggs were all cleaned up.
You're just in time.
Mmmm! These look delicious!
Thanks! Will you help me put up the party decorations at home?
Of course!

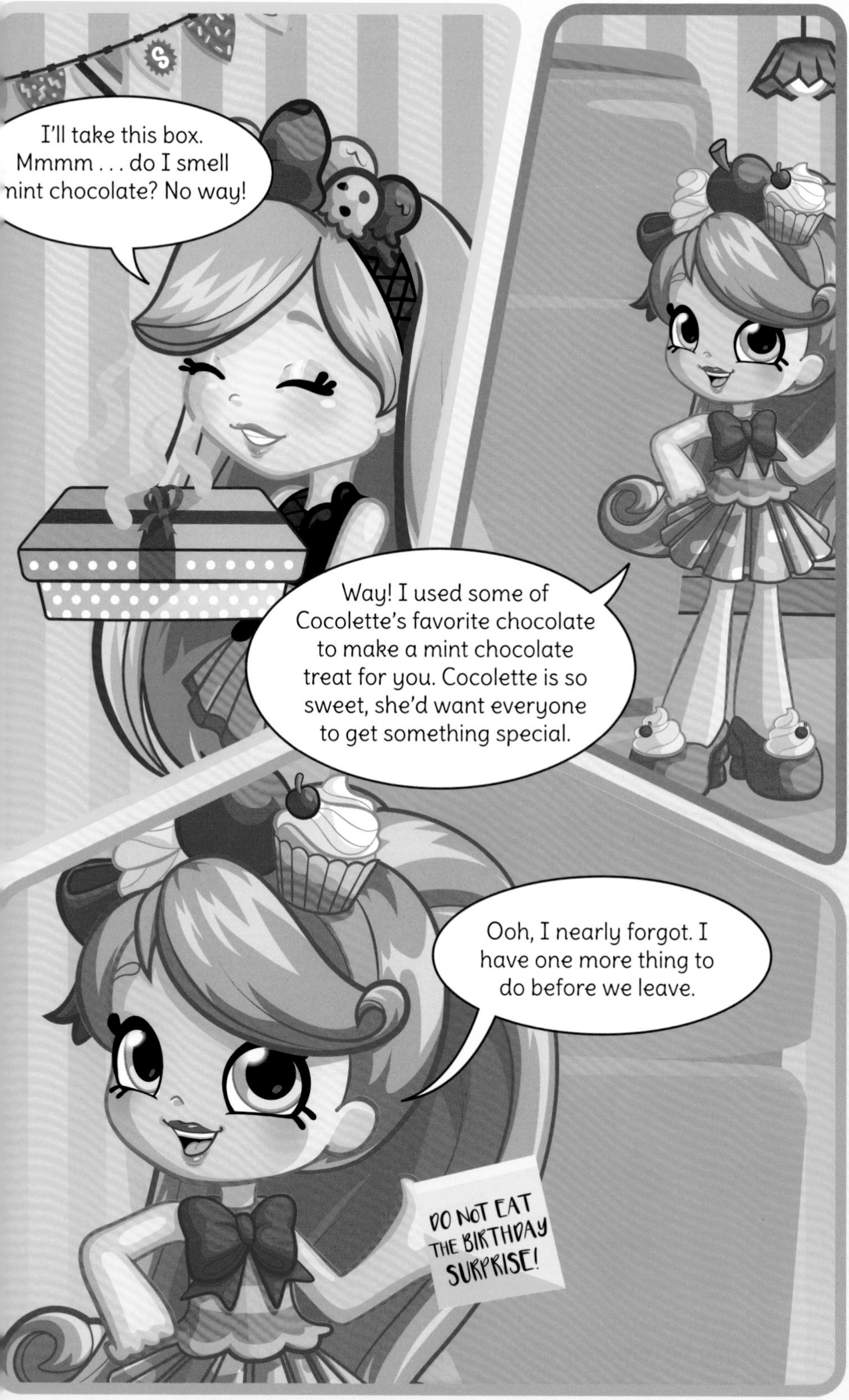
I'll take this box. Mmmm . . . do I smell mint chocolate? No way!
Way! I used some of Cocolette's favorite chocolate to make a mint chocolate treat for you. Cocolette is so sweet, she'd want everyone to get something special.
Ooh, I nearly forgot. I have one more thing to do before we leave.
DO NOT EAT THE BIRTHDAY SURPRISE!

But just at that moment, the birthday girl herself arrived. The friends tried their best to keep Cocolette from discovering the birthday surprises, but they had never been good at keeping secrets.

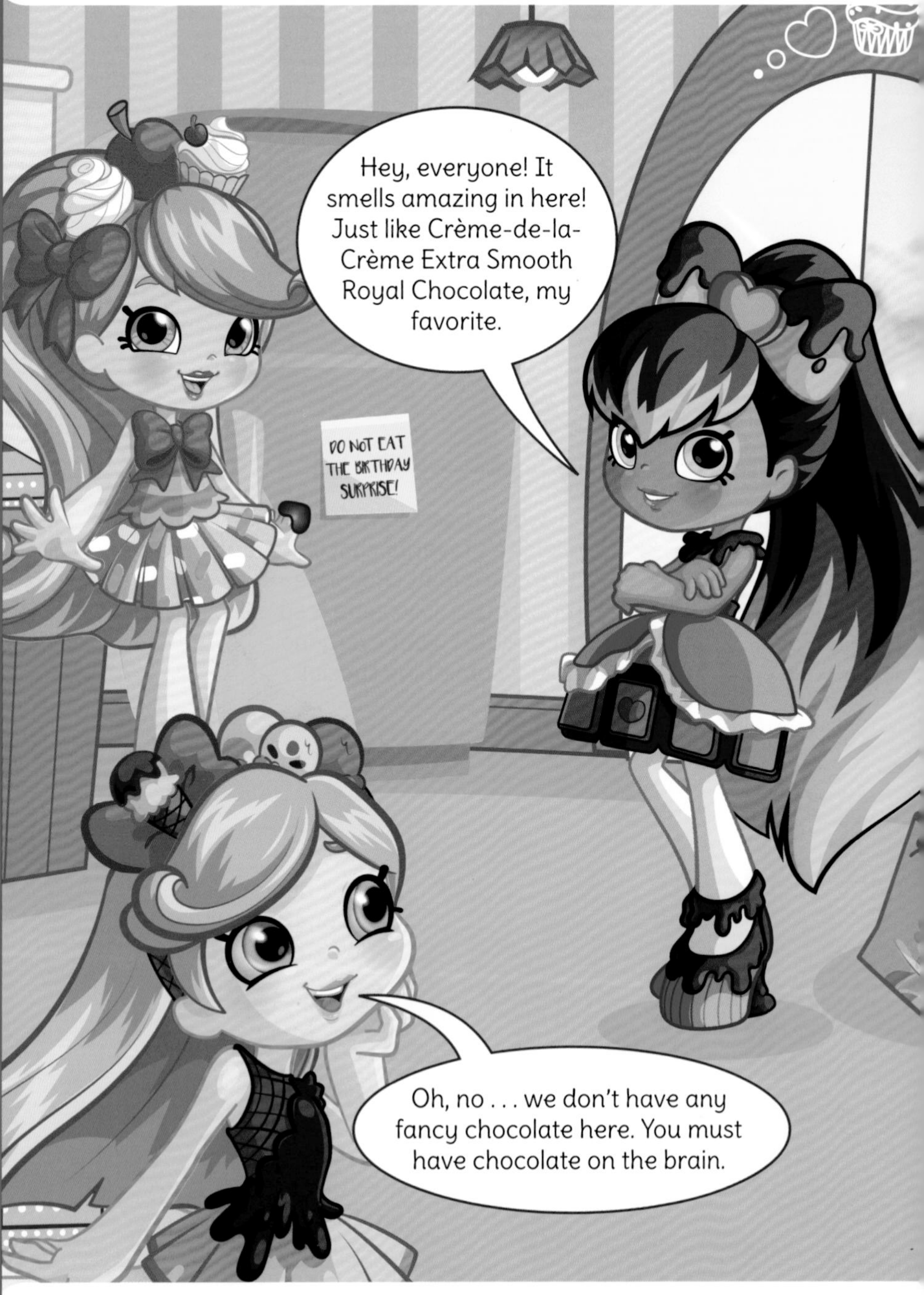

Hey, everyone! It smells amazing in here! Just like Crème-de-la-Crème Extra Smooth Royal Chocolate, my favorite.
DO NOT EAT THE BIRTHDAY SURPRISE!
Oh, no . . . we don't have any fancy chocolate here. You must have chocolate on the brain.

Jessicake and Peppa-Mint tried to hide the cupcakes from Cocolette, but i would only be a matter of time before she noticed the pretty boxes.

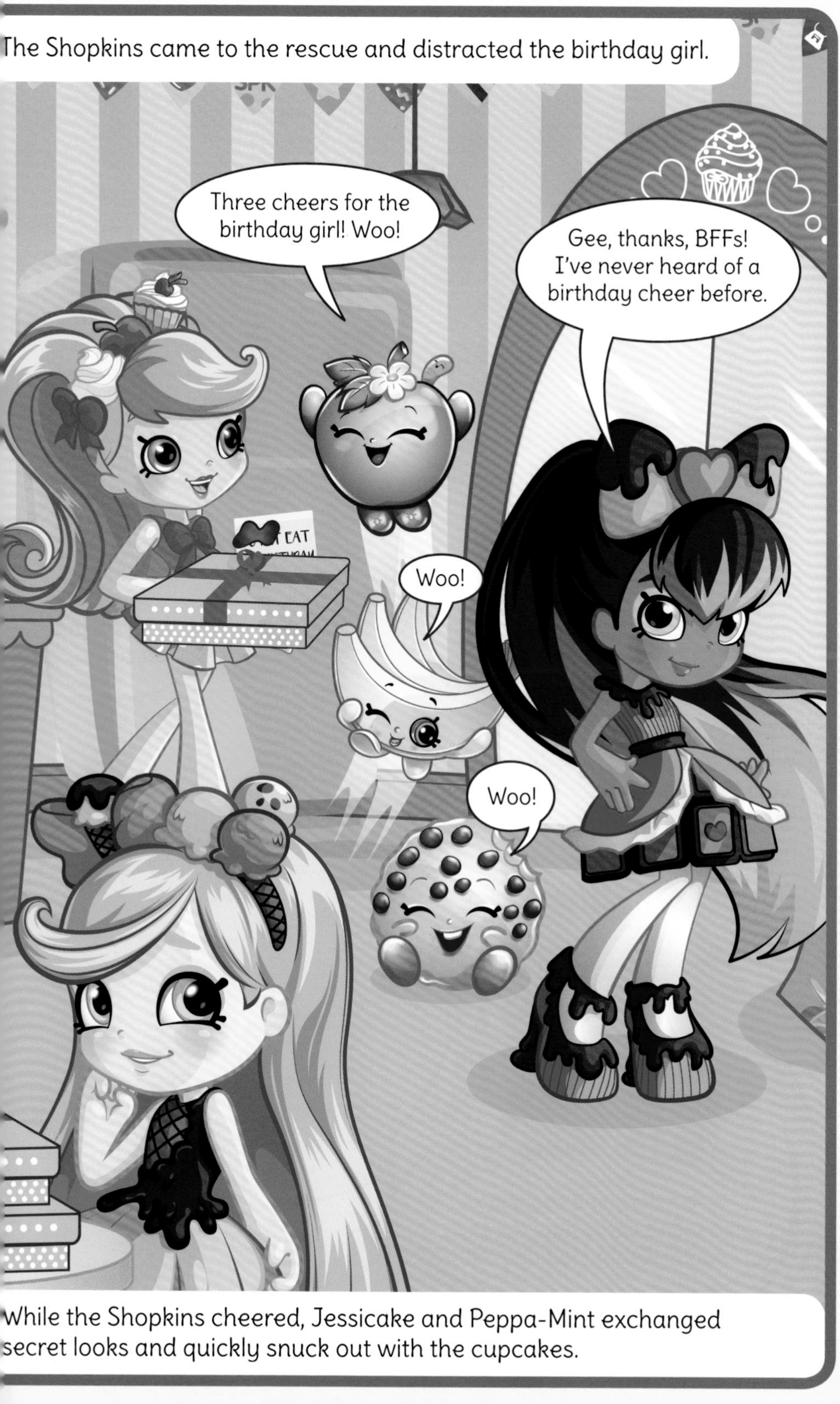
The Shopkins came to the rescue and distracted the birthday girl.
Three cheers for the birthday girl! Woo!
Gee, thanks, BFFs! I've never heard of a birthday cheer before.
Woo!
Woo!
While the Shopkins cheered, Jessicake and Peppa-Mint exchanged secret looks and quickly snuck out with the cupcakes.

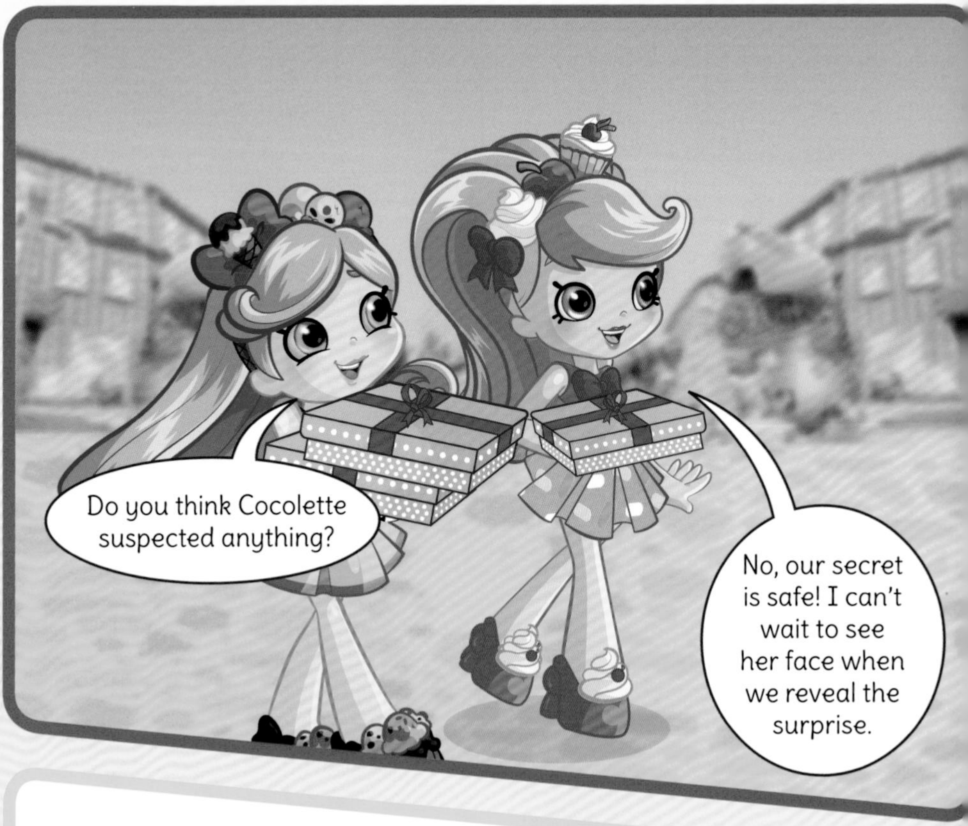
Do you think Cocolette suspected anything?
No, our secret is safe! I can't wait to see her face when we reveal the surprise.

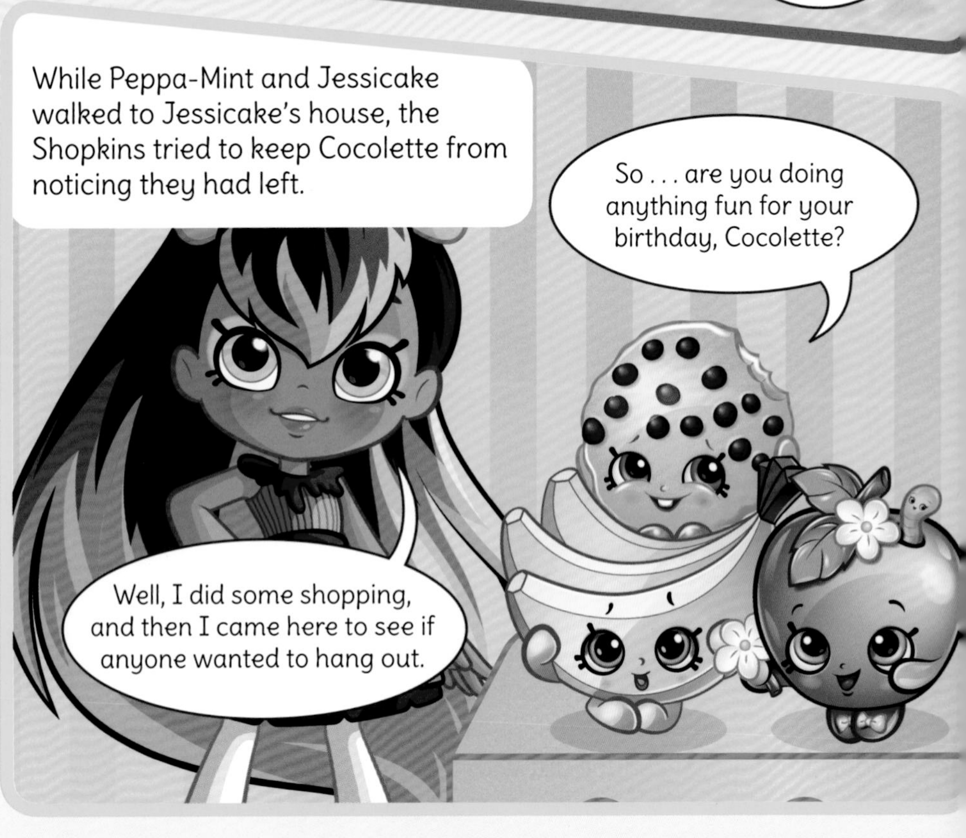
While Peppa-Mint and Jessicake walked to Jessicake's house, the Shopkins tried to keep Cocolette from noticing they had left.
So . . . are you doing anything fun for your birthday, Cocolette?
Well, I did some shopping, and then I came here to see if anyone wanted to hang out.

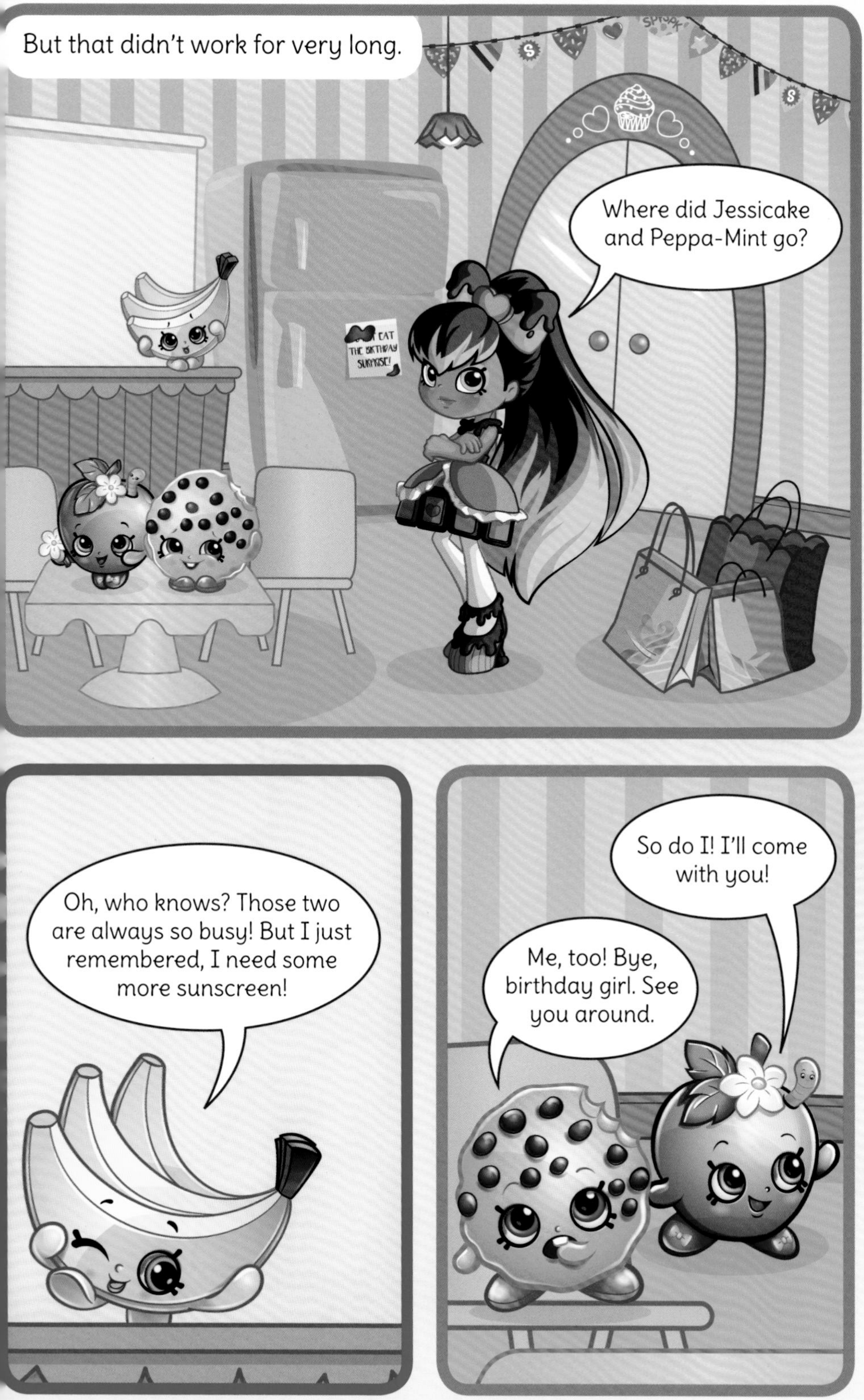
But that didn't work for very long.
Where did Jessicake and Peppa-Mint go?
Oh, who knows? Those two are always so busy! But I just remembered, I need some more sunscreen!
So do I! I'll come with you!
Me, too! Bye, birthday girl. See you around.

Alone in the café, Cocolette worried that her friends were avoiding her. Then she saw something that made her feel better.

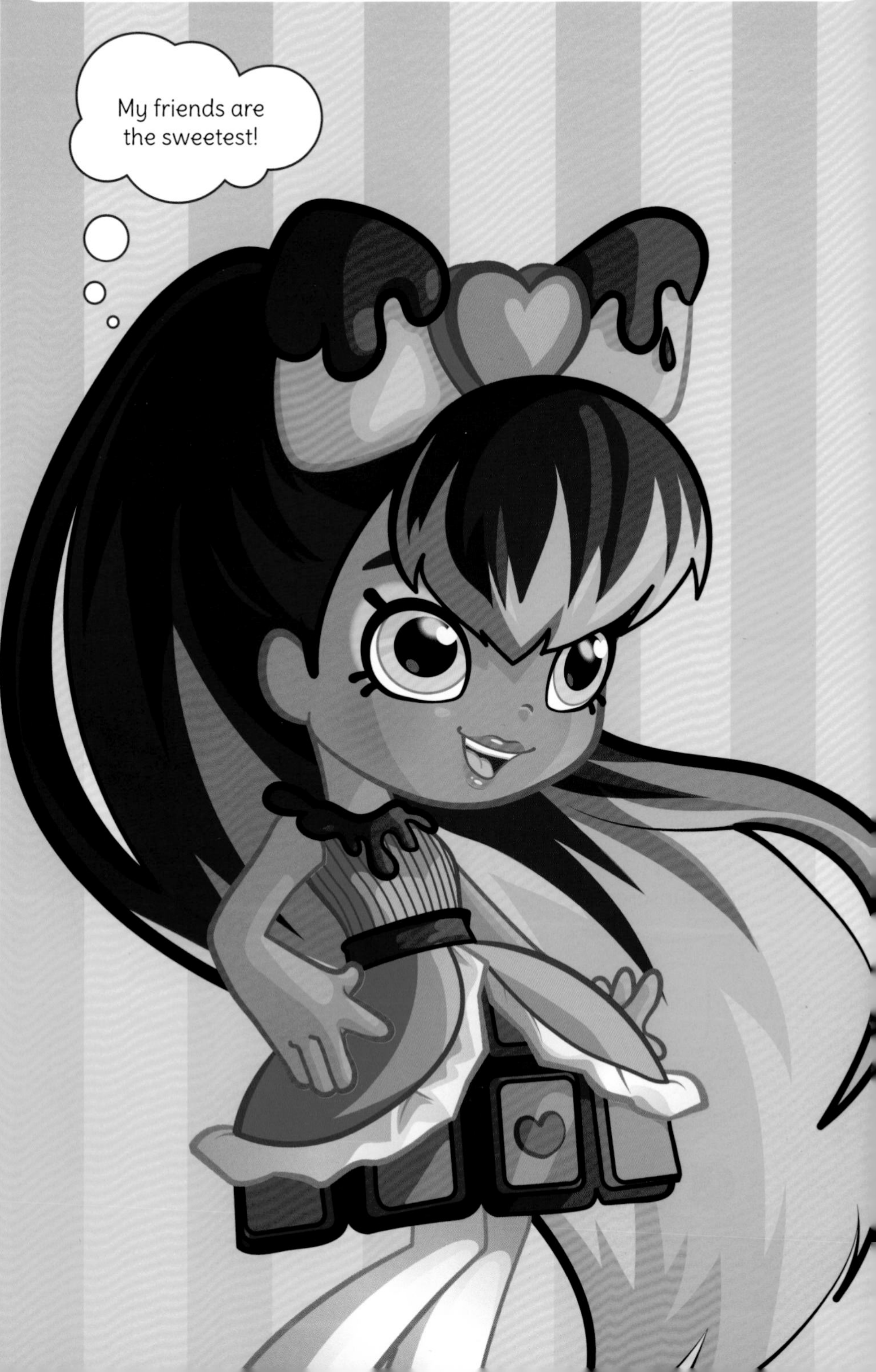
My friends are the sweetest!

When the Shopkins arrived at Jessicake's house, Jessicake and Peppa-Mint were busy, busy, busy preparing for Cocolette's surprise party.

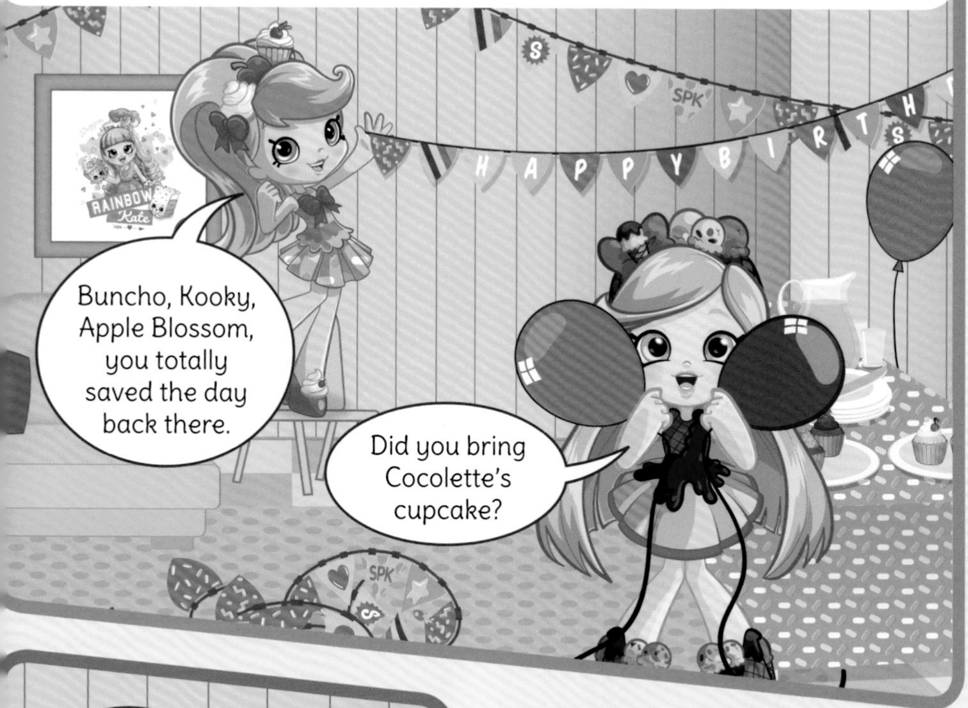
RAINBOW Kate
Buncho, Kooky, Apple Blossom, you totally saved the day back there.
Did you bring Cocolette's cupcake?

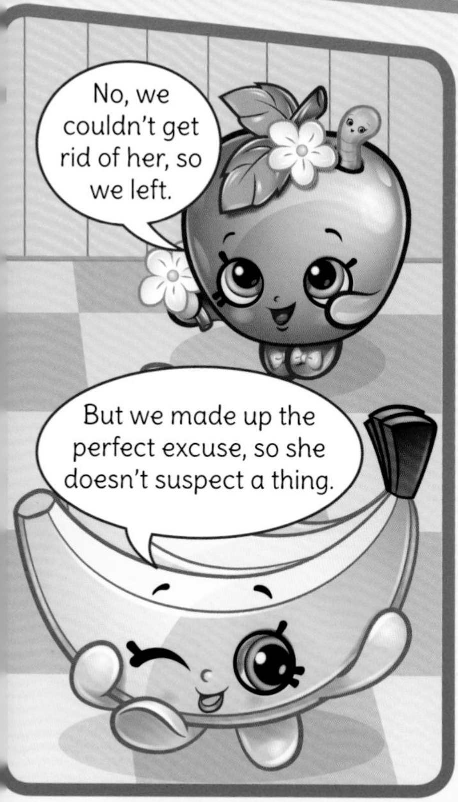
No, we couldn't get rid of her, so we left.
But we made up the perfect excuse, so she doesn't suspect a thing.

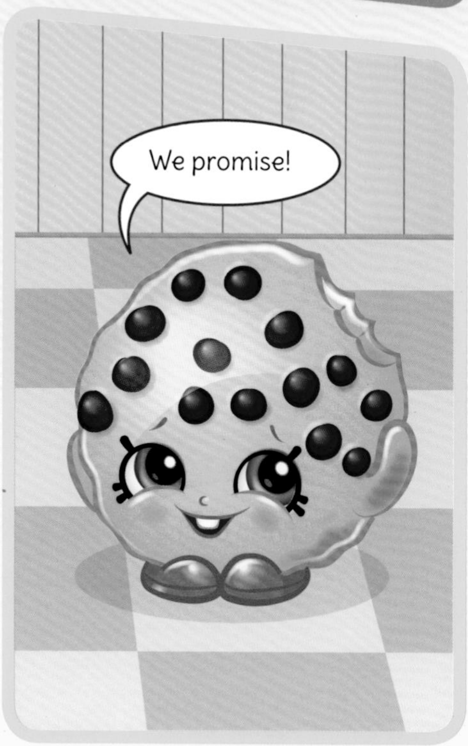
We promise!

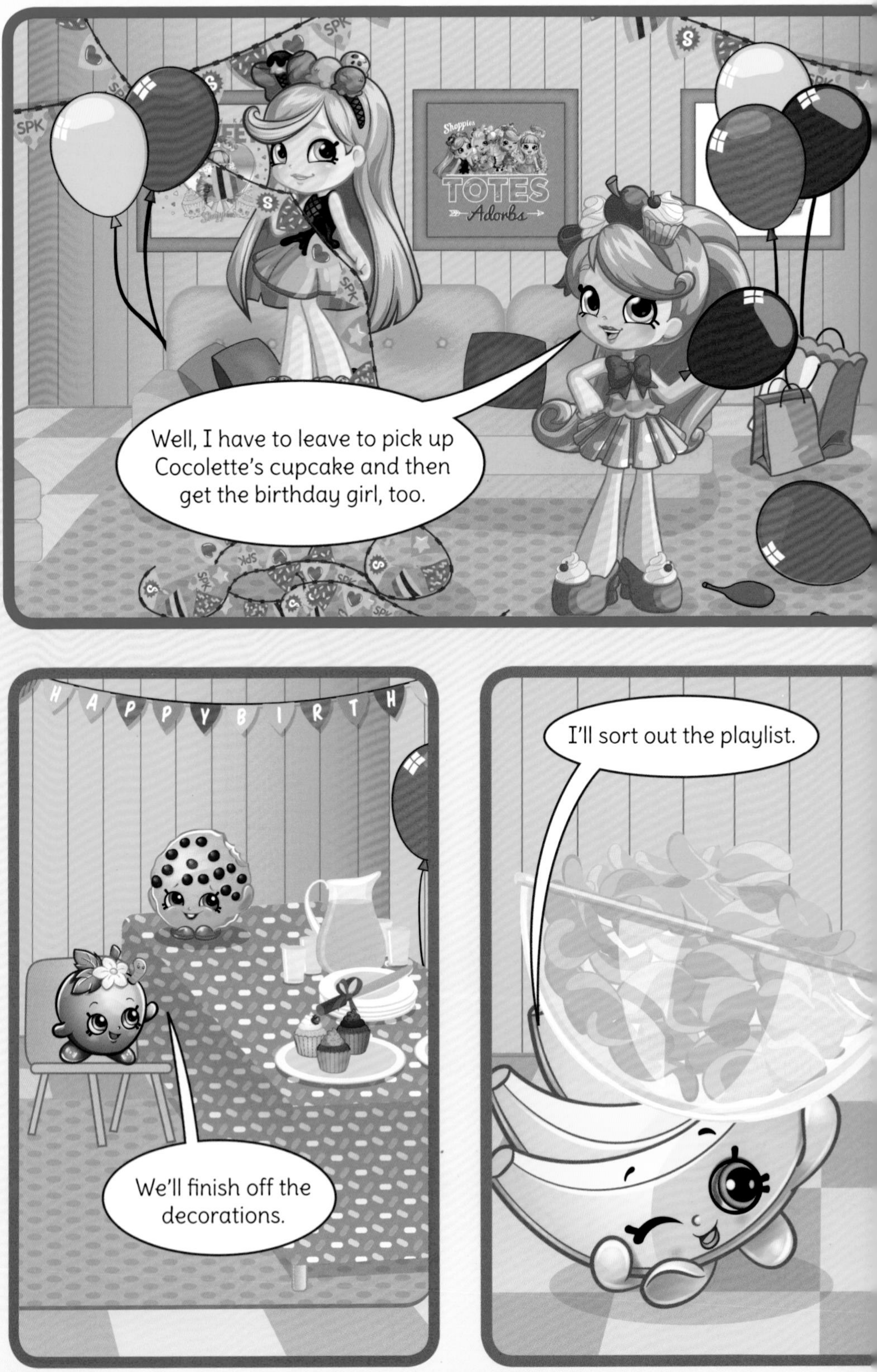
TOTES
Adorbs
Well, I have to leave to pick up Cocolette's cupcake and then get the birthday girl, too.
HAPPYBIRTH
We'll finish off the decorations.
I'll sort out the playlist.

Jessicake arrived back at the Cupcake Queen Café, but it wasn't the way she had left it!

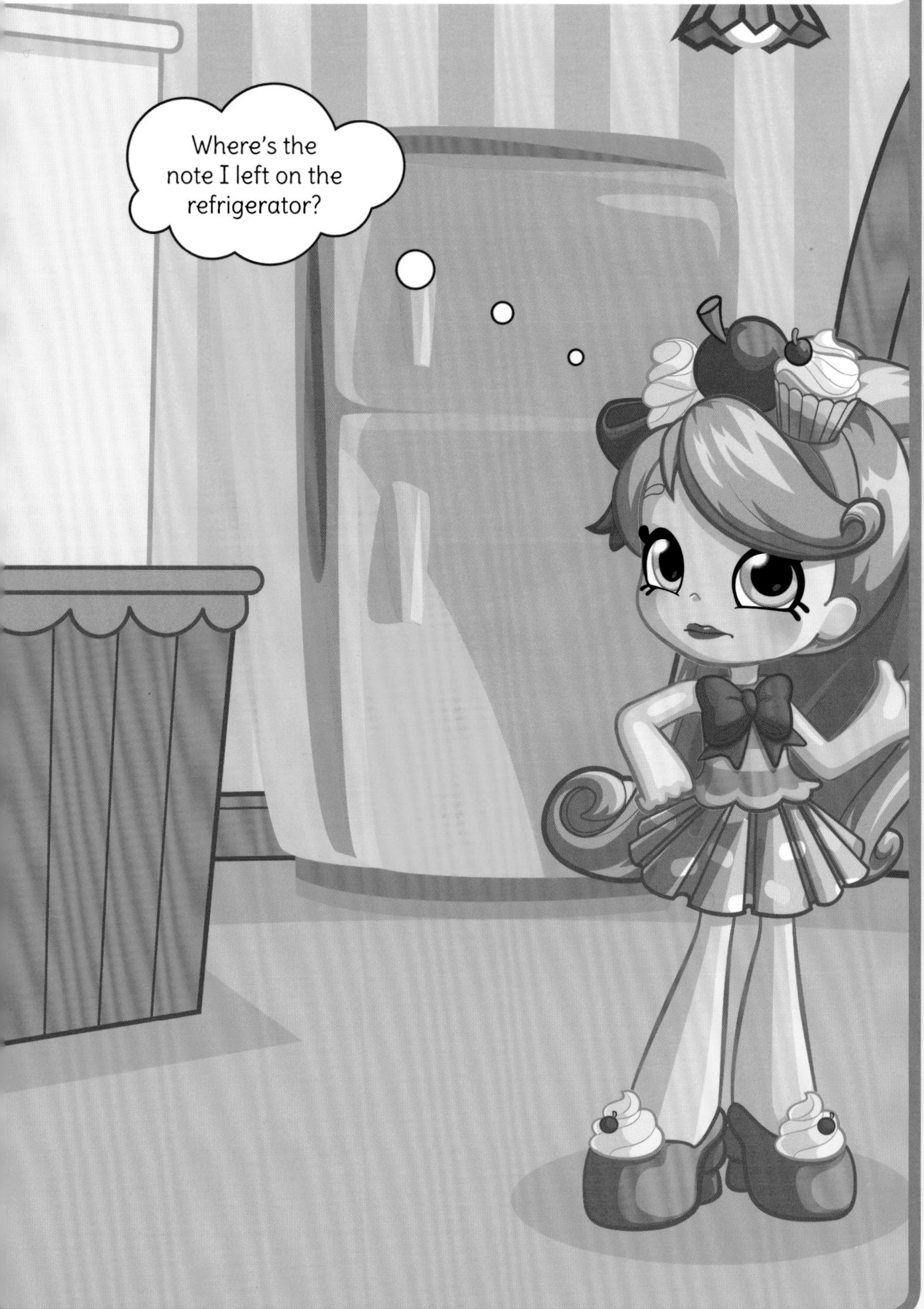
Where's the note I left on the refrigerator?

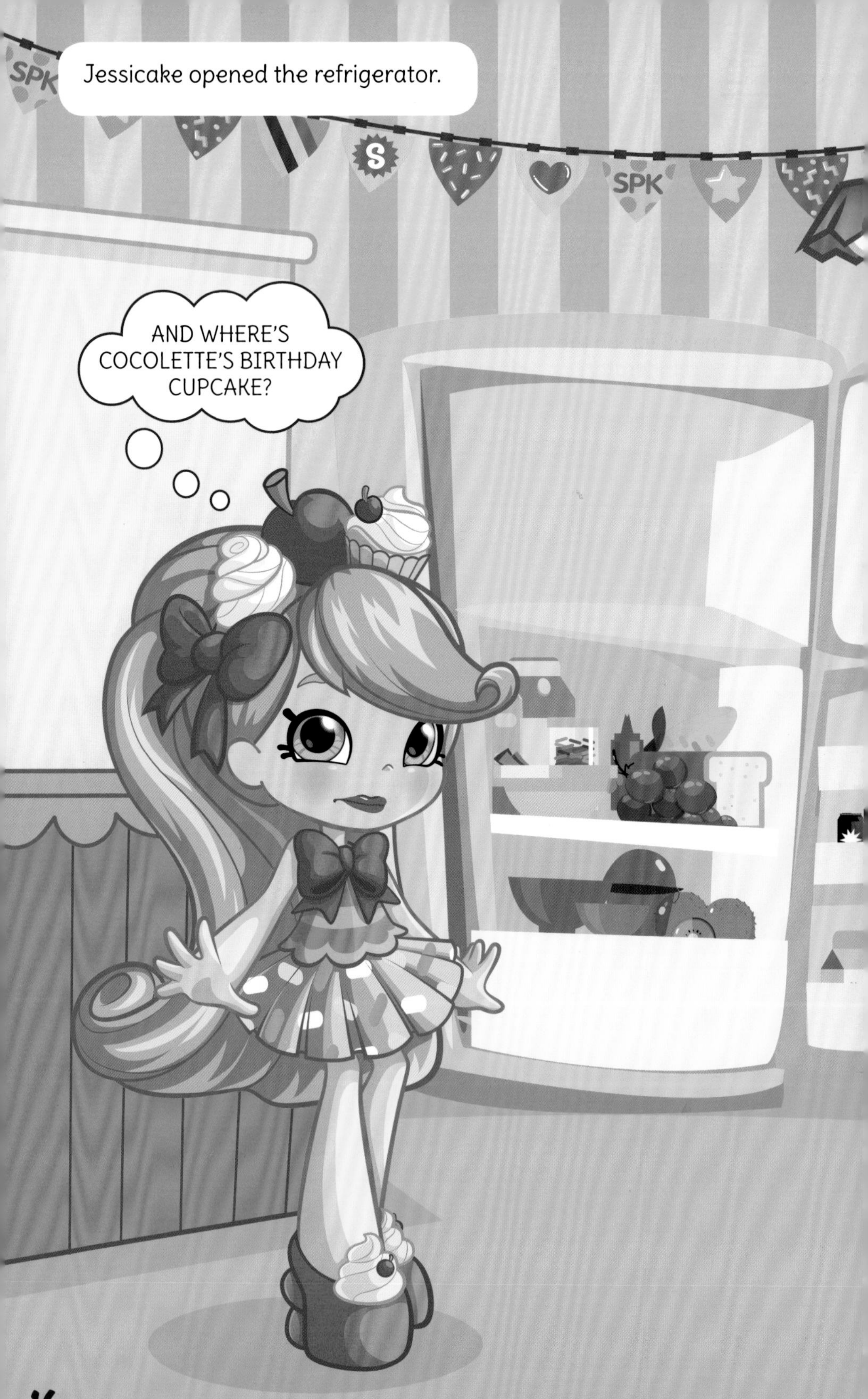
Jessicake opened the refrigerator.
AND WHERE'S COCOLETTE'S BIRTHDAY CUPCAKE?

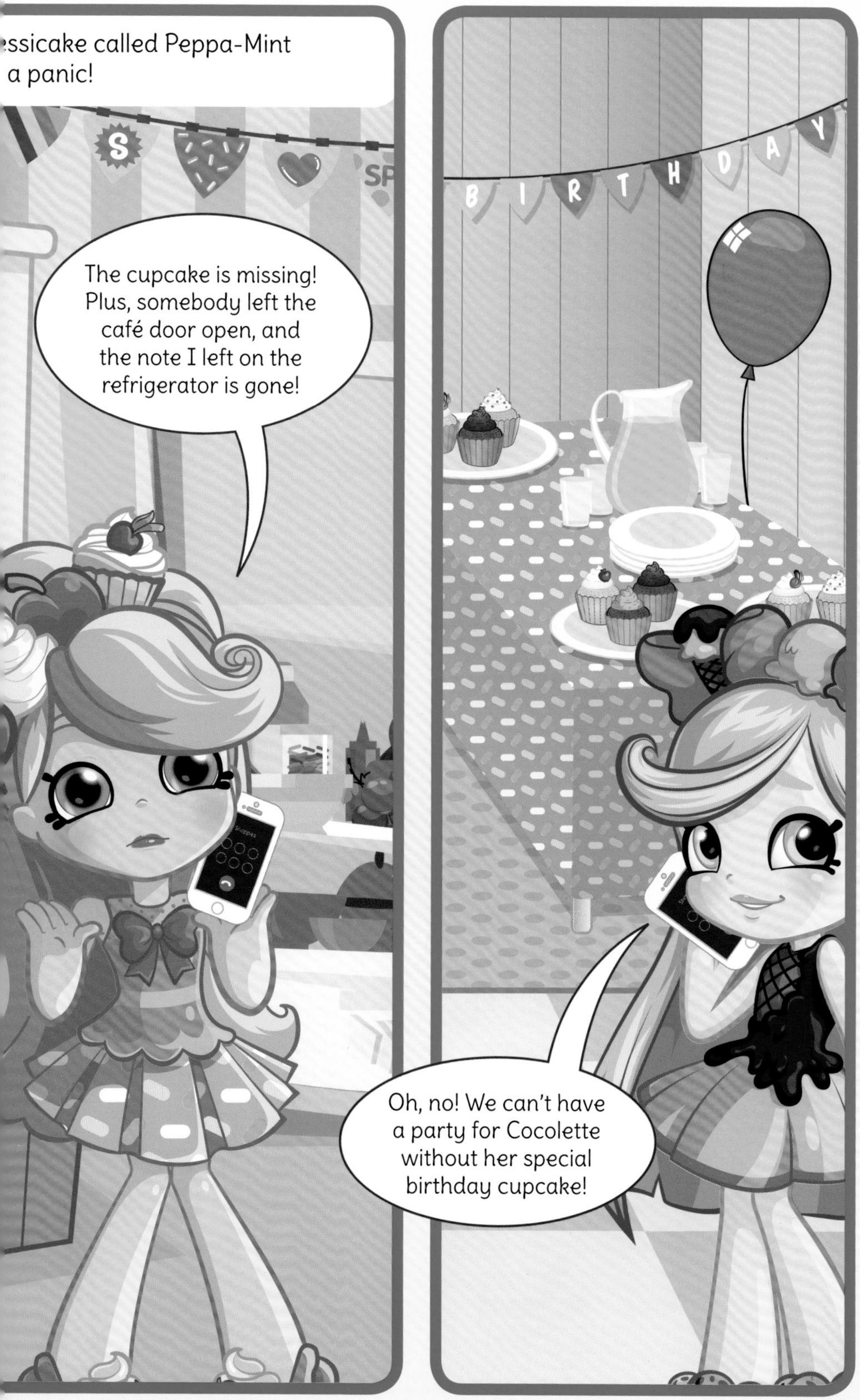
ssicake called Peppa-Mint
a panic!
The cupcake is missing! Plus, somebody left the café door open, and the note I left on the refrigerator is gone!
BIRTHDAY
Oh, no! We can't have a party for Cocolette without her special birthday cupcake!

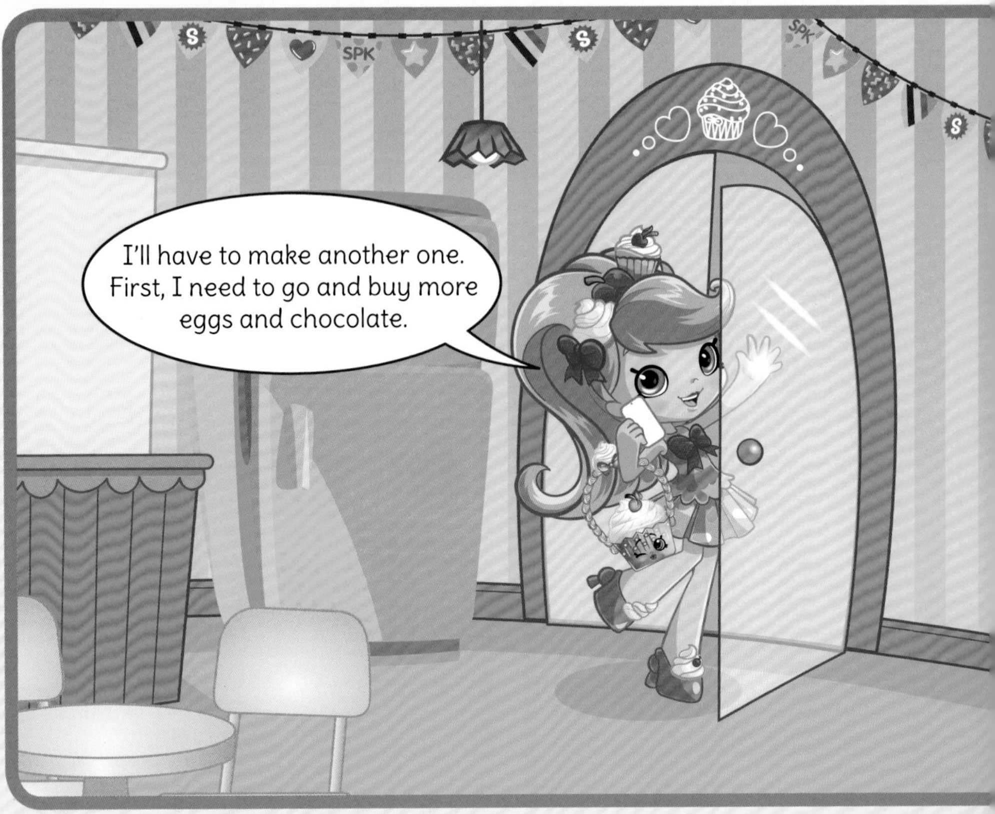
I'll have to make another one. First, I need to go and buy more eggs and chocolate.

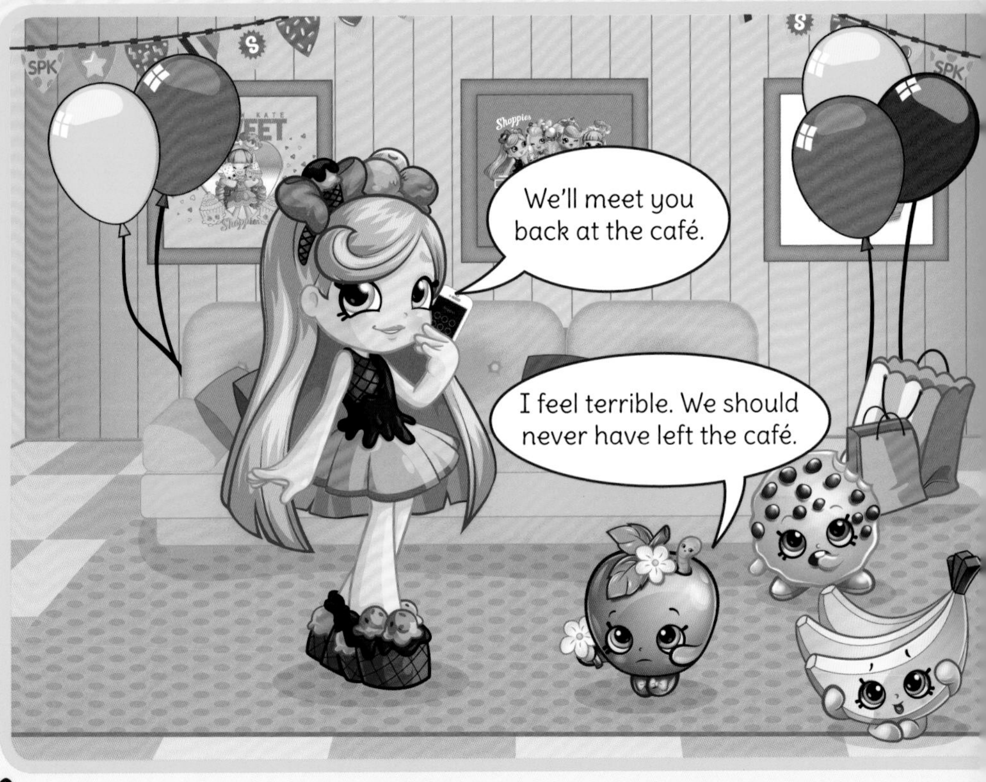
We'll meet you back at the café.
I feel terrible. We should never have left the café.

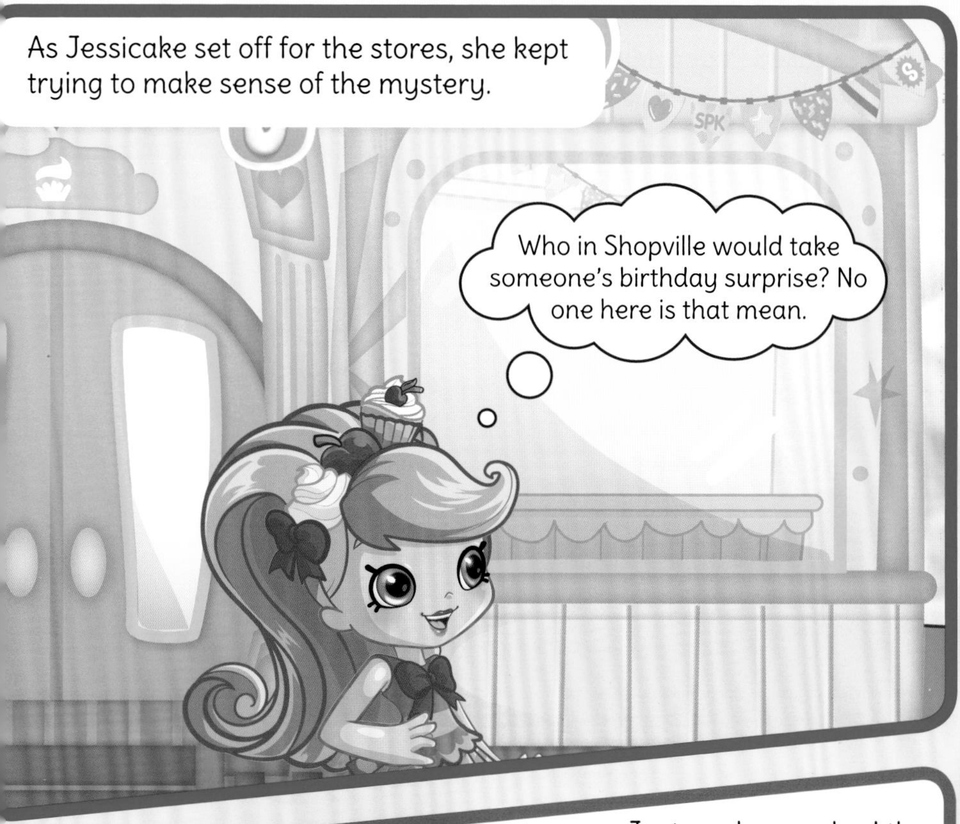
As Jessicake set off for the stores, she kept trying to make sense of the mystery.
Who in Shopville would take someone's birthday surprise? No one here is that mean.

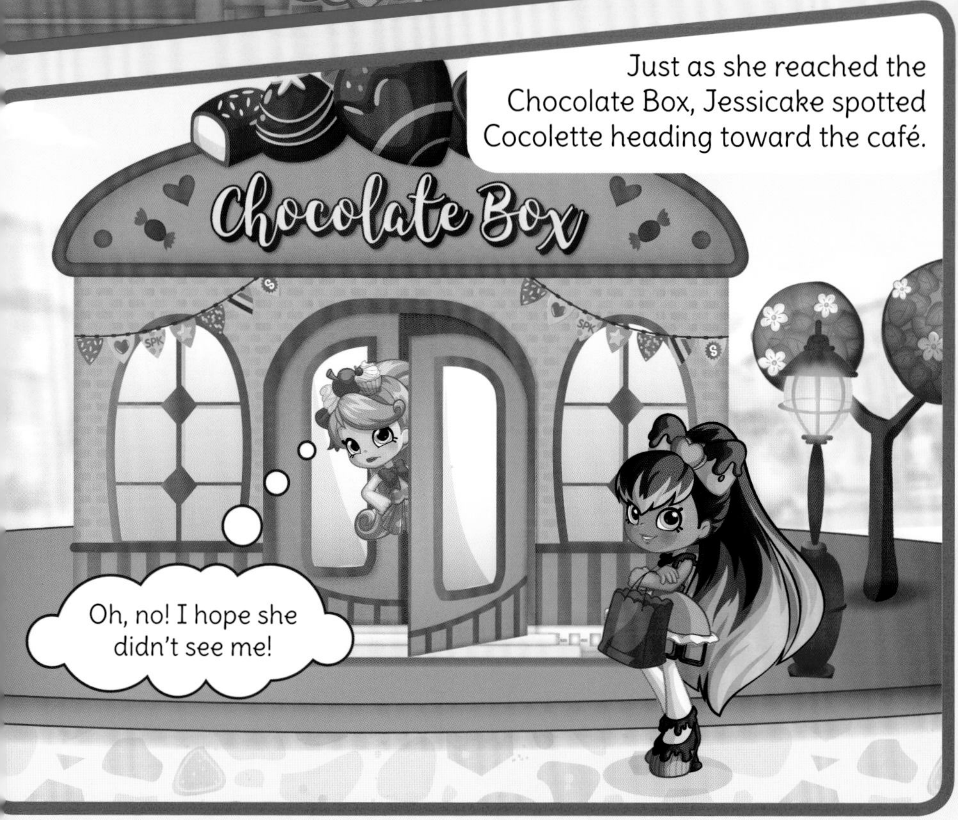
Just as she reached the Chocolate Box, Jessicake spotted Cocolette heading toward the café.
Chocolate Box
SPK
SPK
Oh, no! I hope she didn't see me!

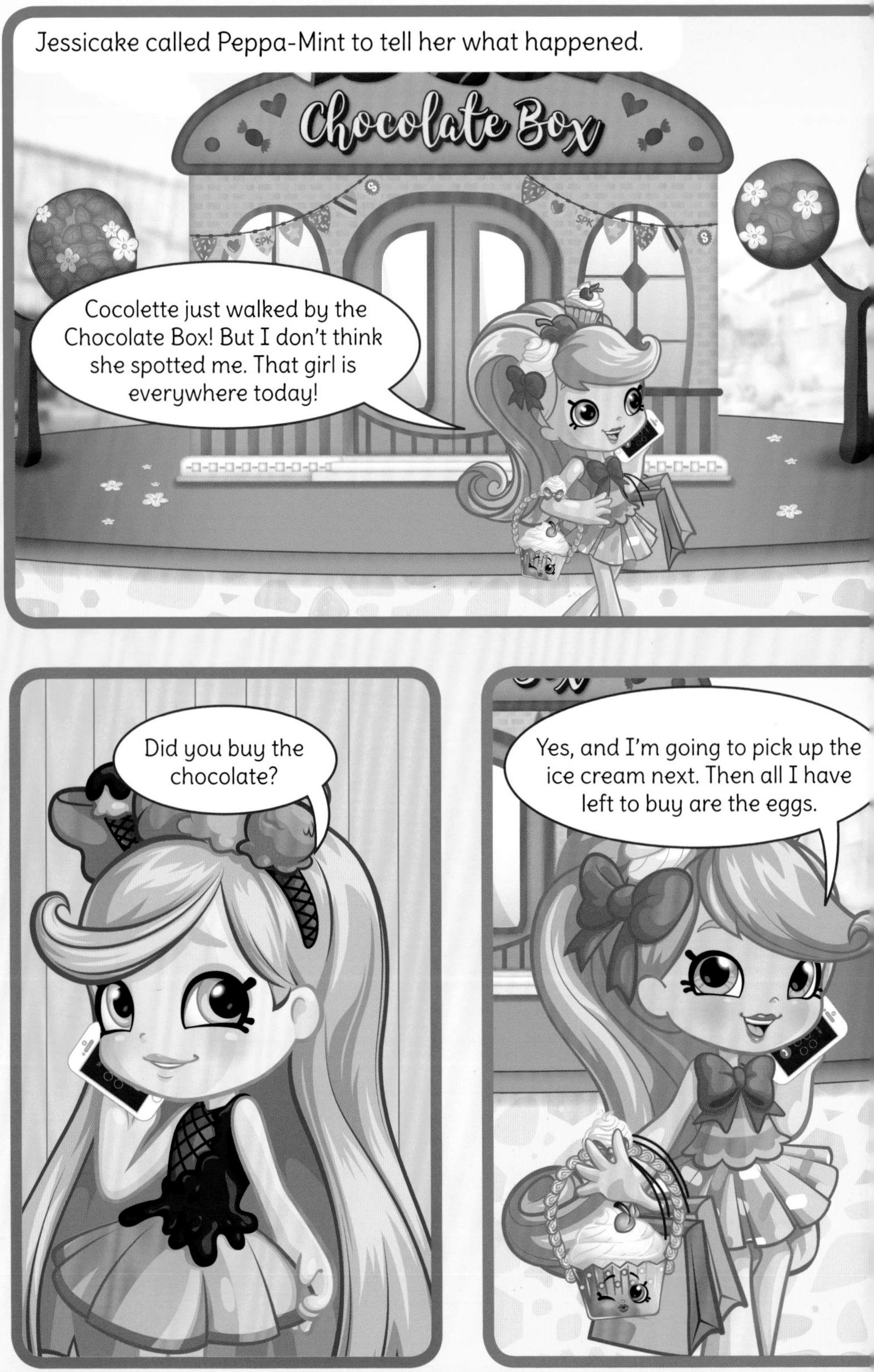
Jessicake called Peppa-Mint to tell her what happened.
Chocolate Box
Cocolette just walked by the Chocolate Box! But I don't think she spotted me. That girl is everywhere today!
Did you buy the chocolate?
Yes, and I'm going to pick up the ice cream next. Then all I have left to buy are the eggs.

At the Small Mart, Jessicake approached the aisle where the eggs were kept, and she discovered some bad news.

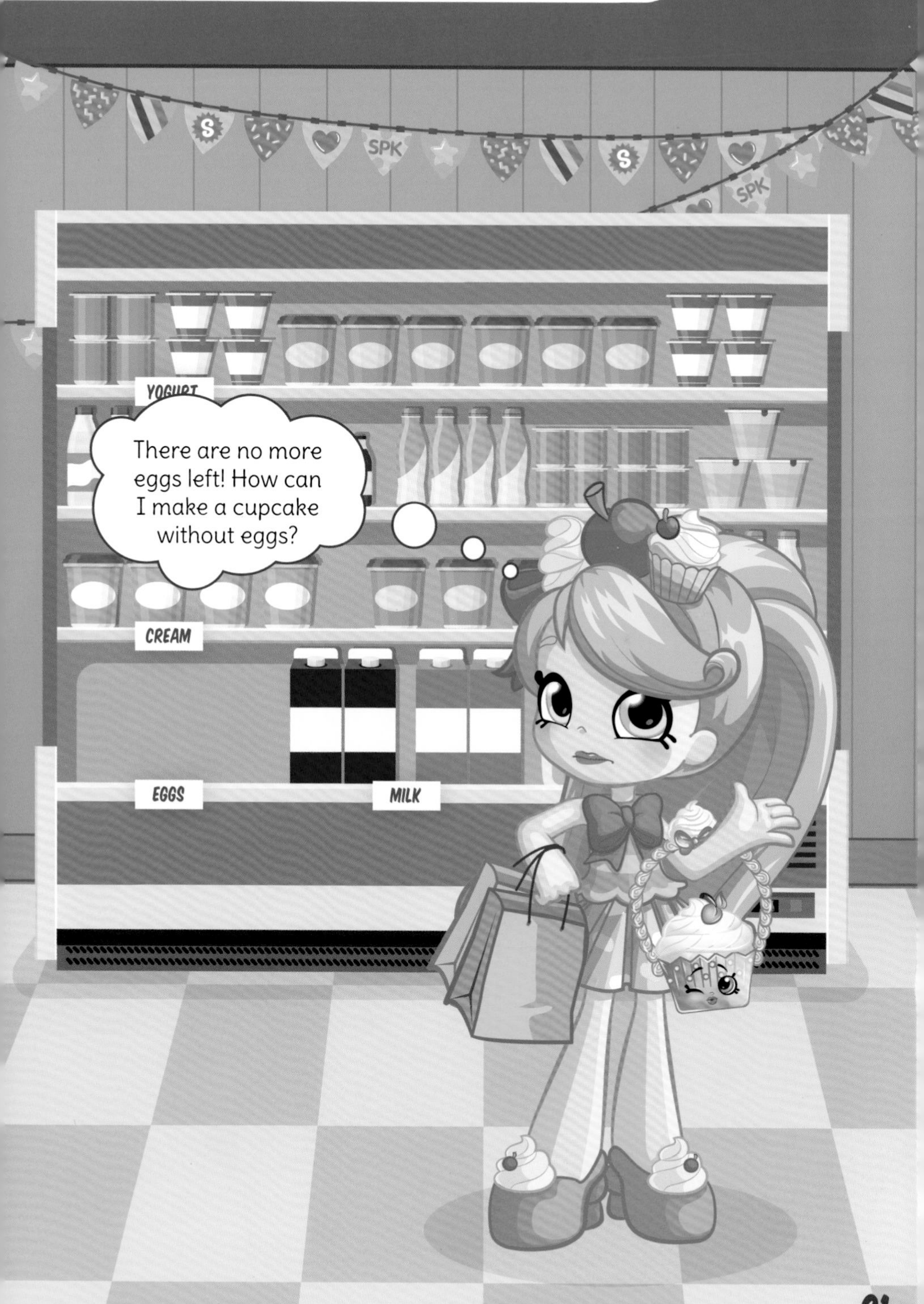
There are no more eggs left! How can I make a cupcake without eggs?
YOGURT
CREAM
EGGS
MILK
SPK

On their way back to the Cupcake Queen Café, Peppa-Mint and the Shopkins tried to figure out who could be behind the mystery of the missing cupcake.

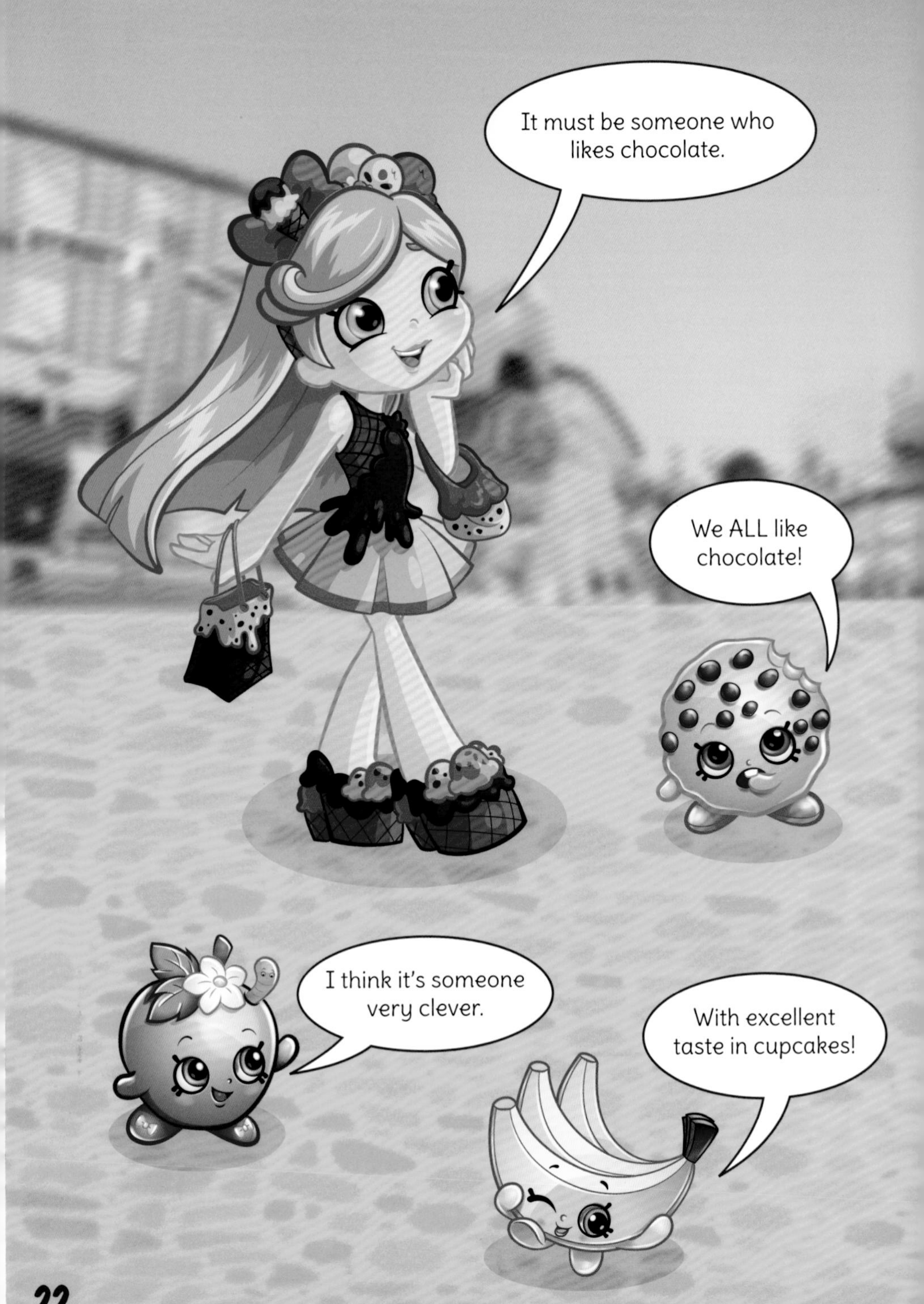
It must be someone who likes chocolate.
We ALL like chocolate!
I think it's someone very clever.
With excellent taste in cupcakes!

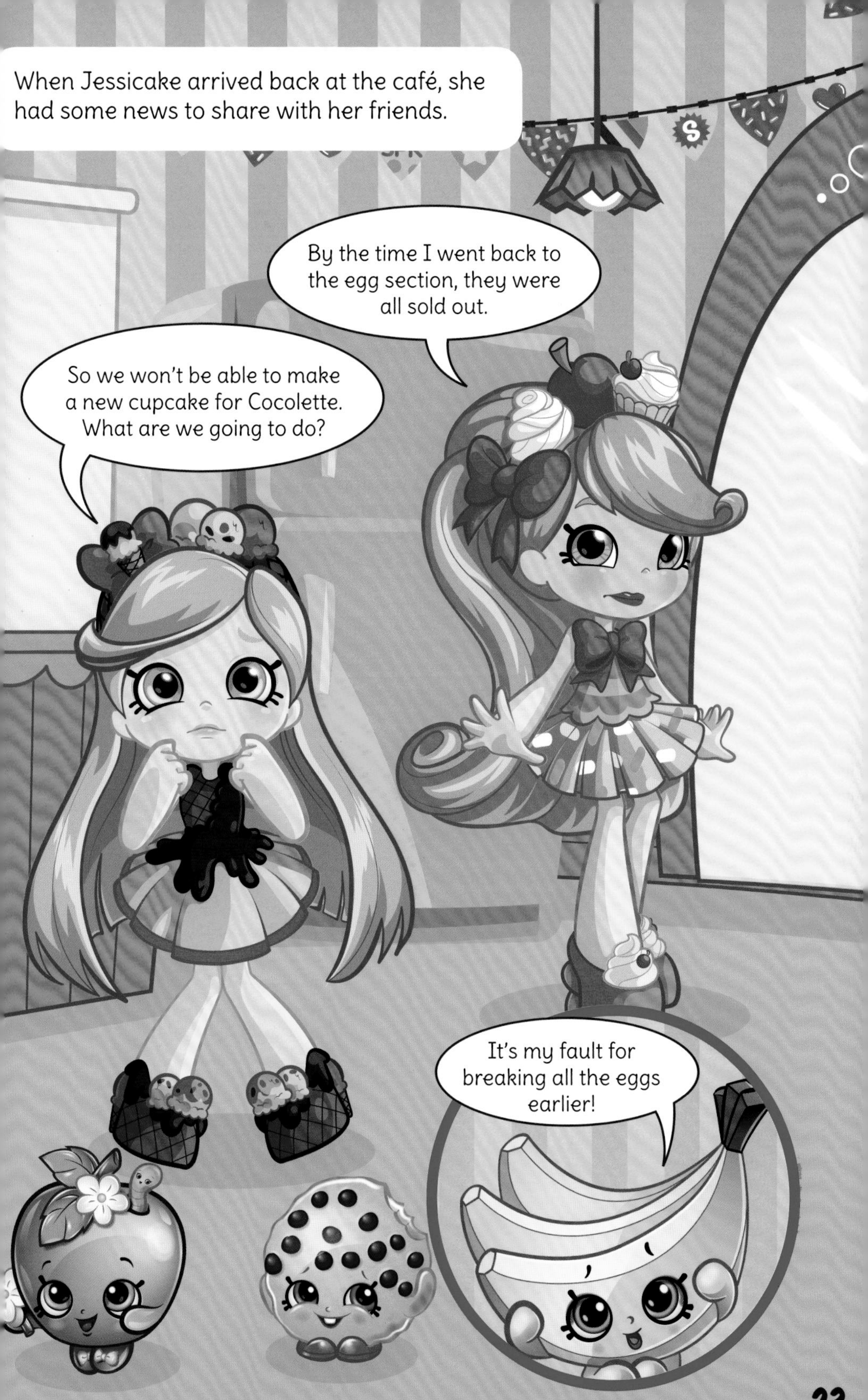
When Jessicake arrived back at the café, she had some news to share with her friends.
By the time I went back to the egg section, they were all sold out.
So we won't be able to make a new cupcake for Cocolette. What are we going to do?
It's my fault for breaking all the eggs earlier!

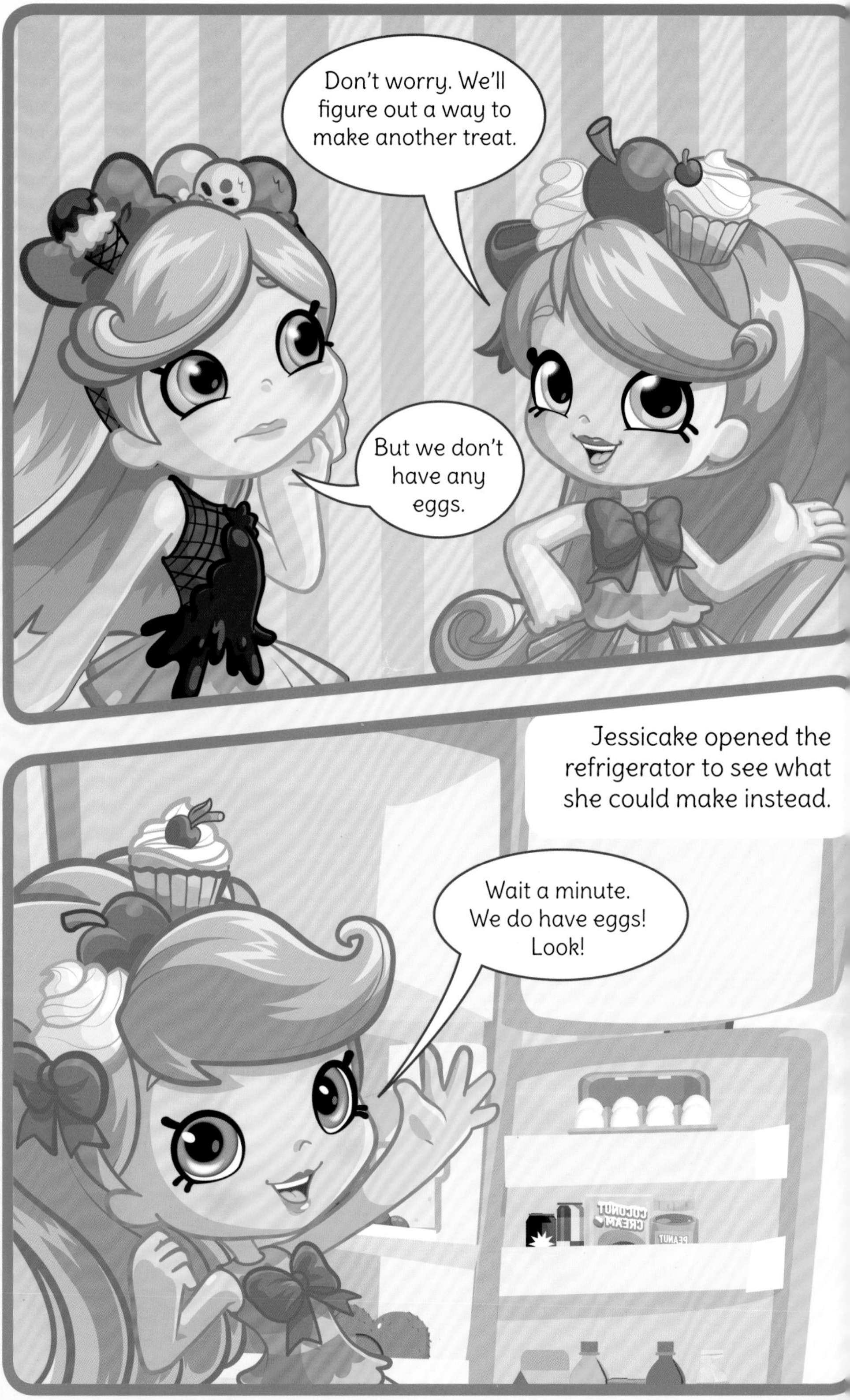
Don't worry. We'll figure out a way to make another treat.
But we don't have any eggs.
Jessicake opened the refrigerator to see what she could make instead.
Wait a minute. We do have eggs! Look!

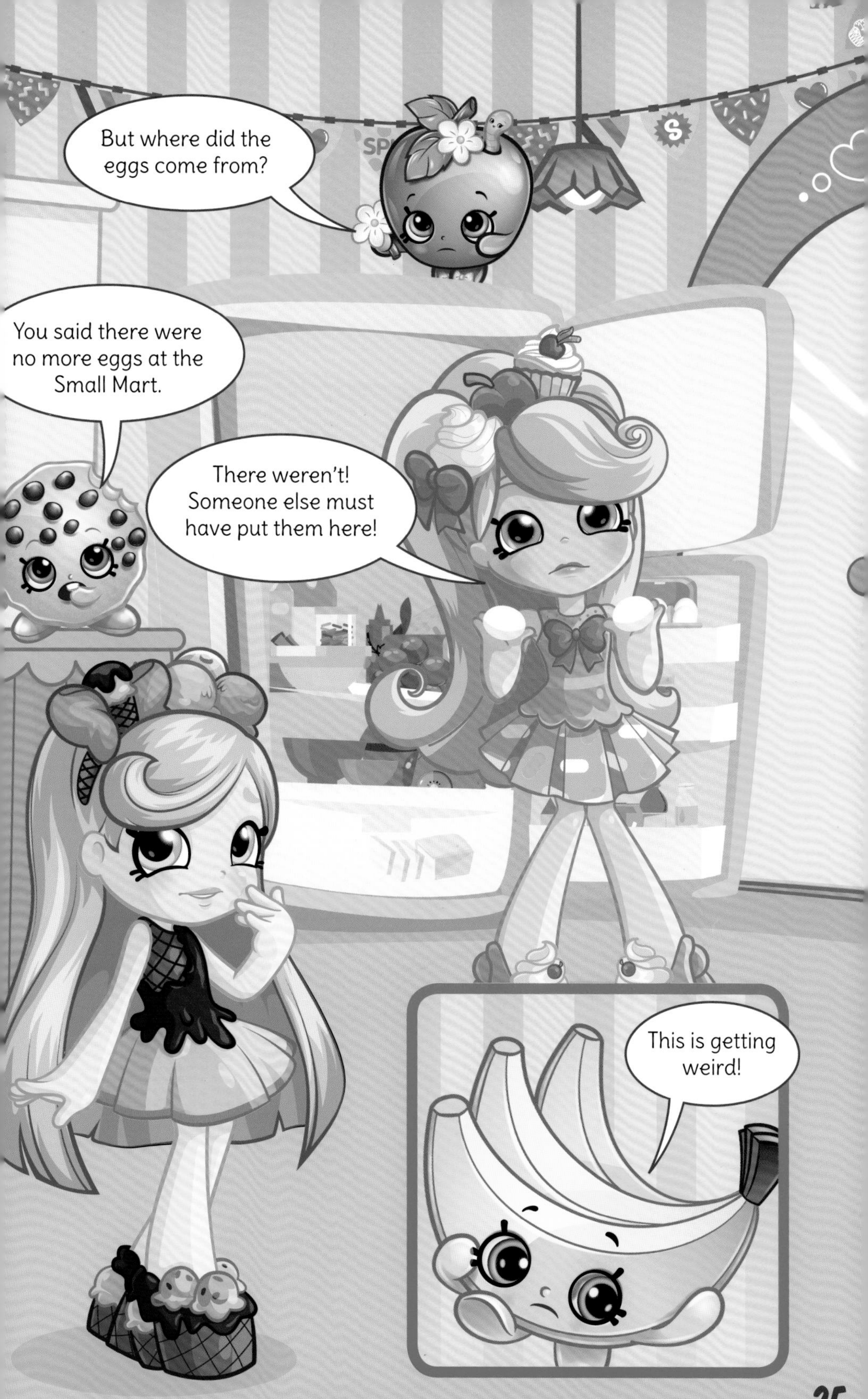
But where did the eggs come from?
You said there were no more eggs at the Small Mart.
There weren't! Someone else must have put them here!
This is getting weird!

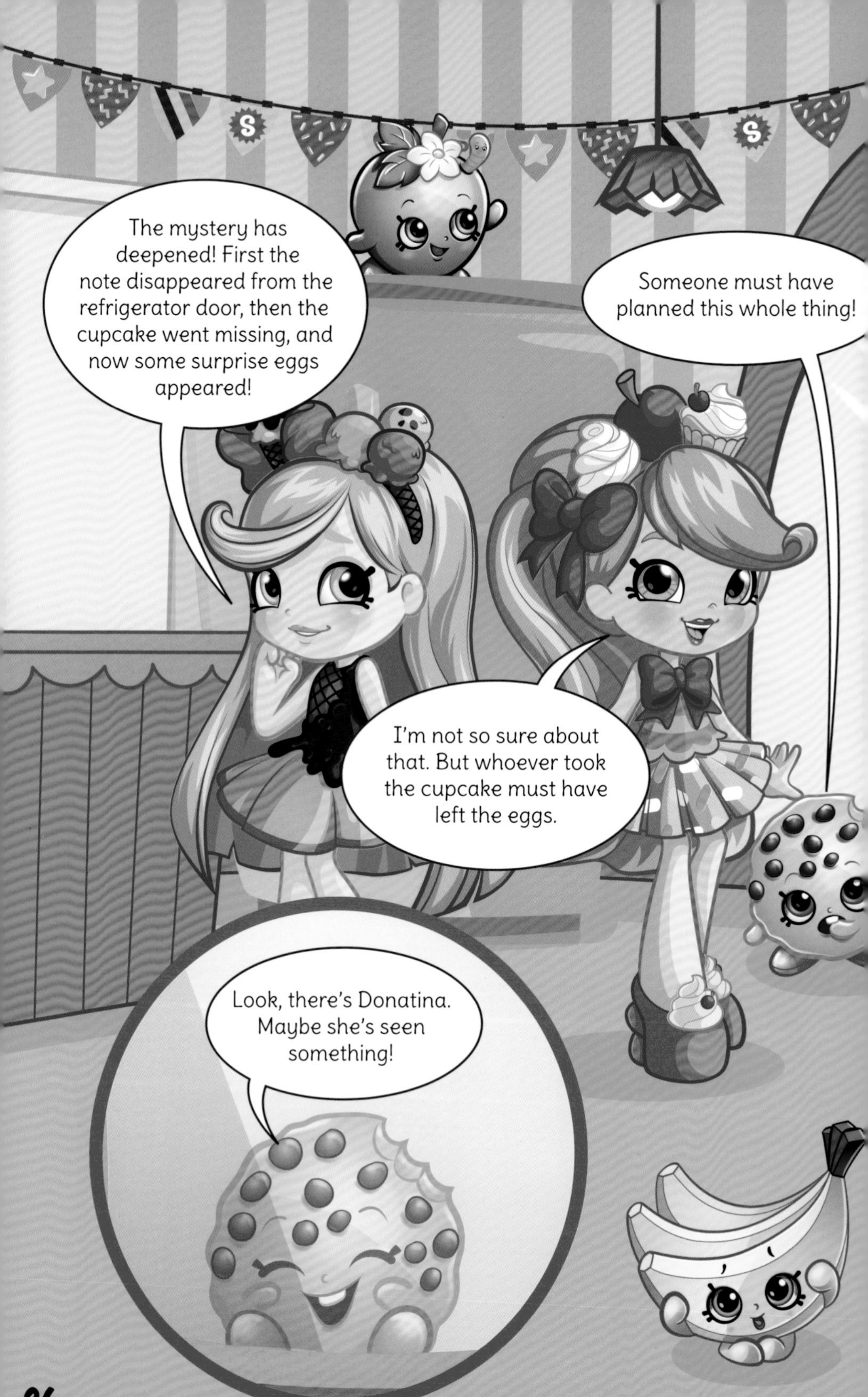
The mystery has deepened! First the note disappeared from the refrigerator door, then the cupcake went missing, and now some surprise eggs appeared!
Someone must have planned this whole thing!
I'm not so sure about that. But whoever took the cupcake must have left the eggs.
Look, there's Donatina. Maybe she's seen something!

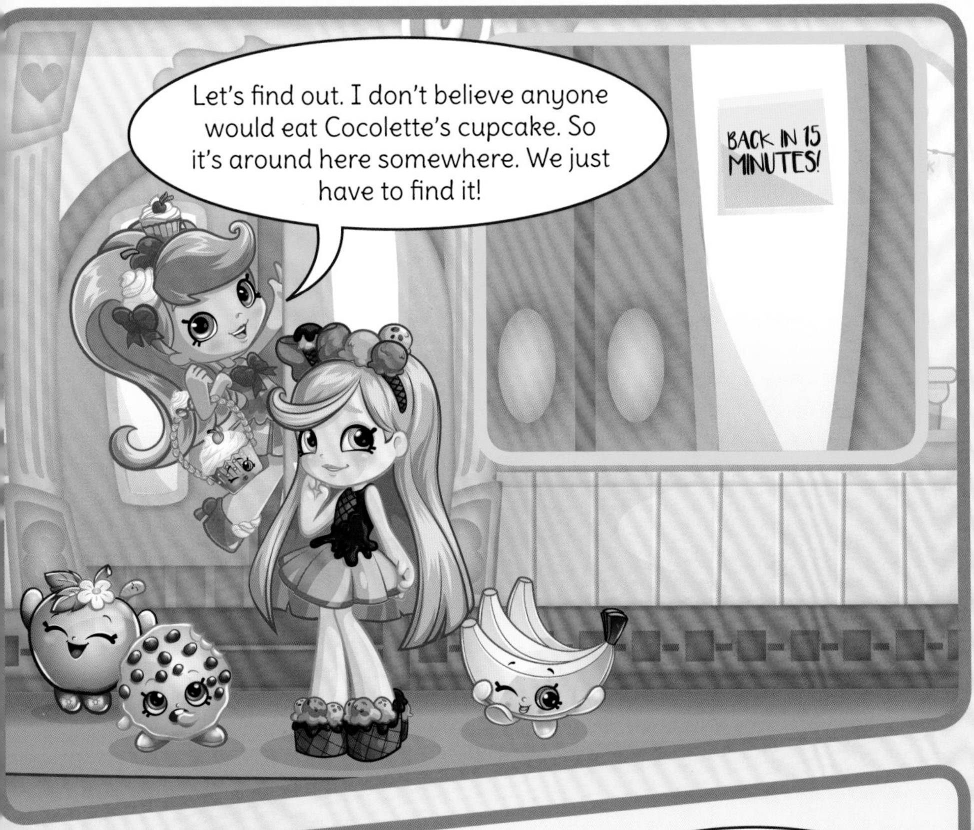
Let's find out. I don't believe anyone would eat Cocolette's cupcake. So it's around here somewhere. We just have to find it!
BACK IN 15 MINUTES!

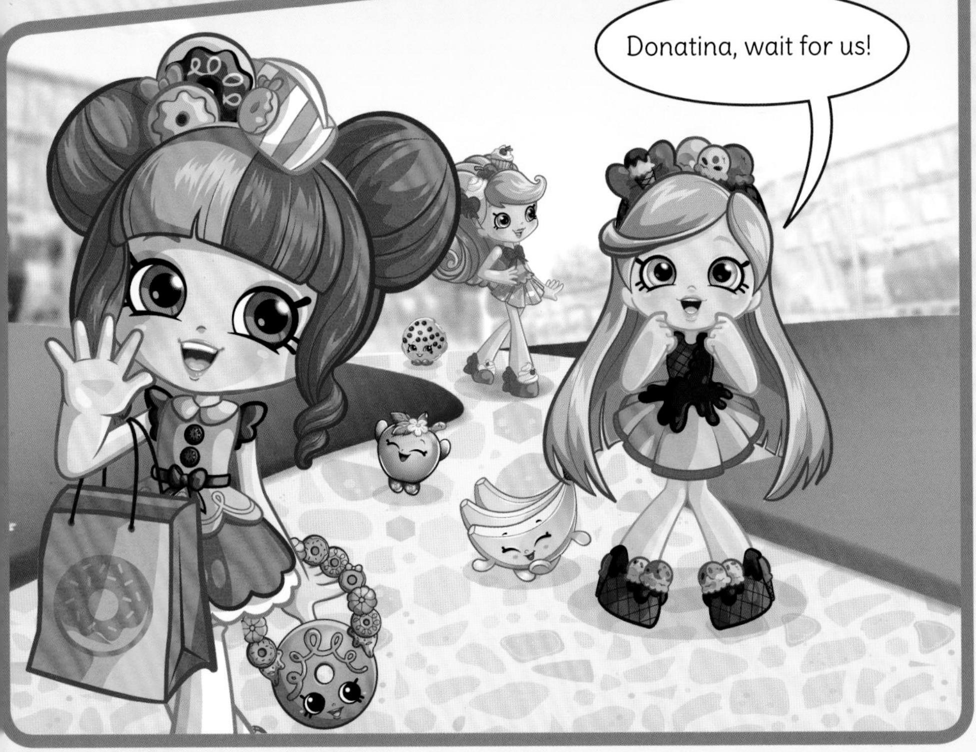
Donatina, wait for us!

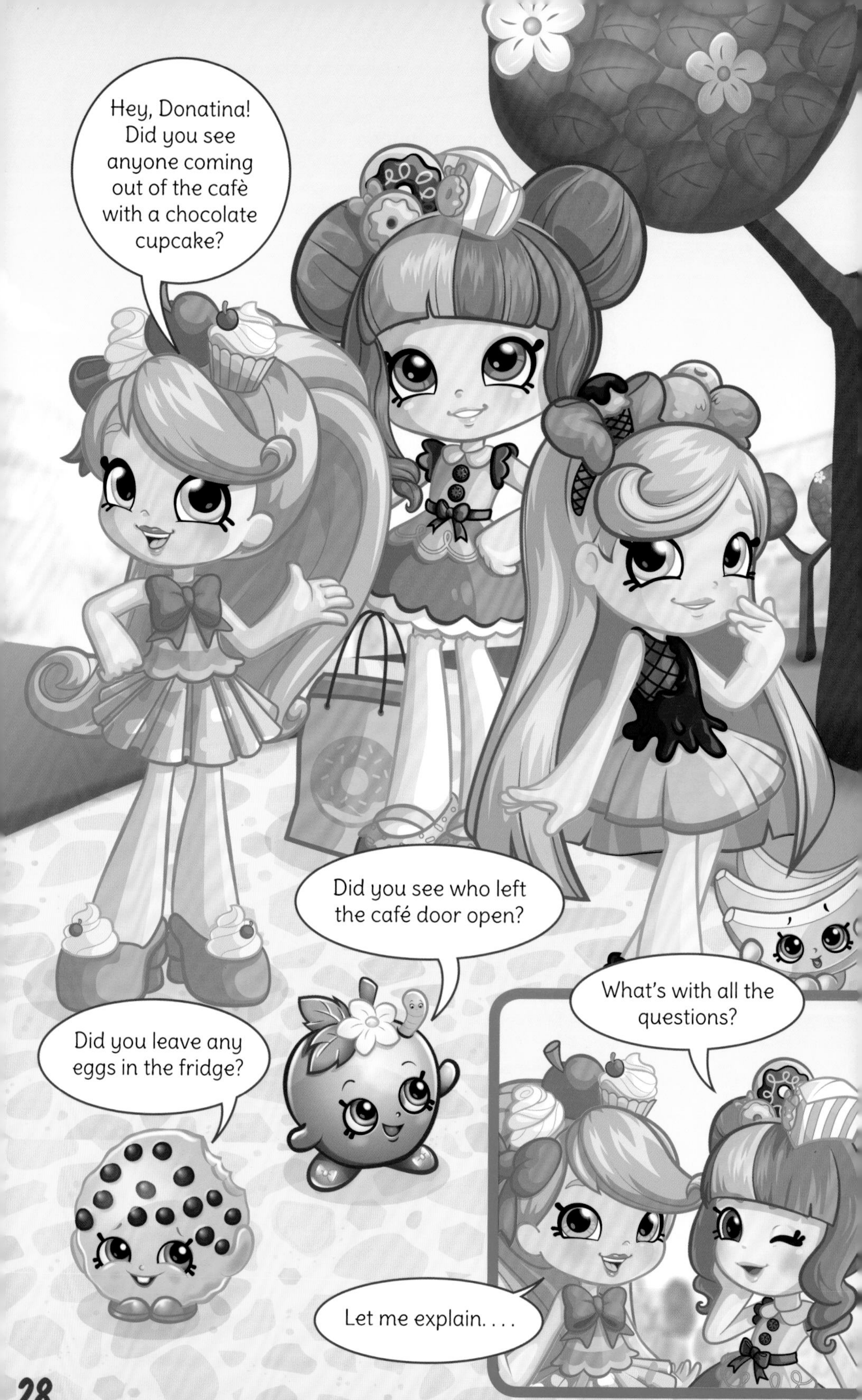
Hey, Donatina! Did you see anyone coming out of the cafè with a chocolate cupcake?
Did you see who left the café door open?
Did you leave any eggs in the fridge?
What's with all the questions?
Let me explain. . . .

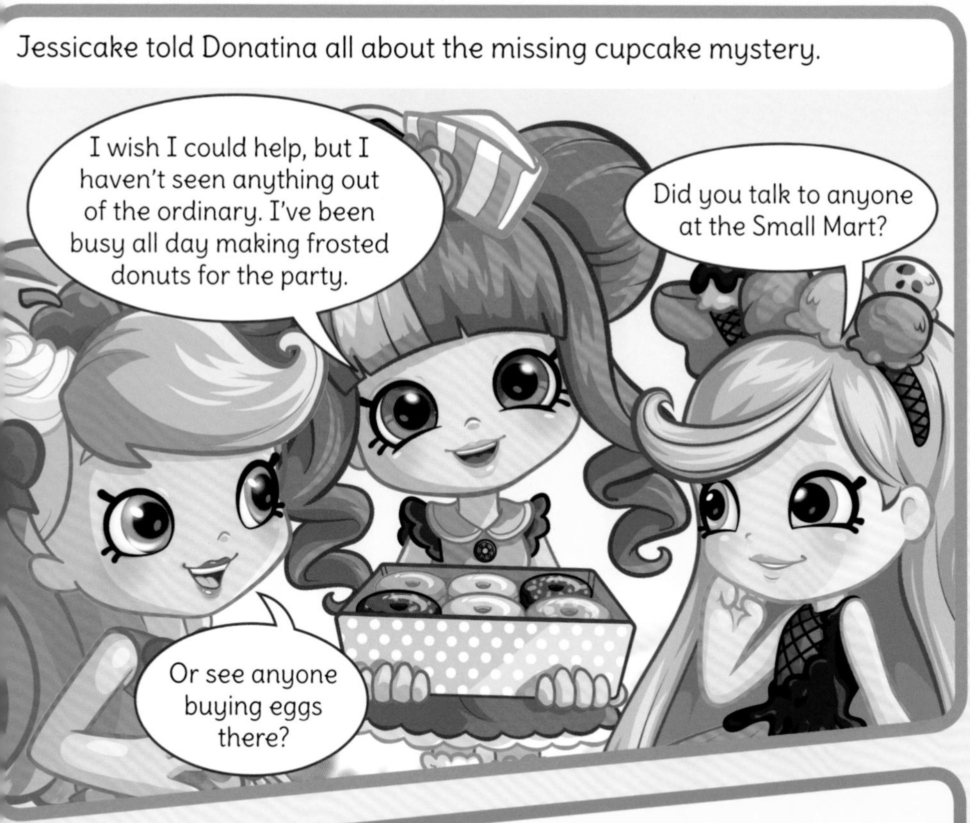
Jessicake told Donatina all about the missing cupcake mystery.
I wish I could help, but I haven't seen anything out of the ordinary. I've been busy all day making frosted donuts for the party.
Did you talk to anyone at the Small Mart?
Or see anyone buying eggs there?

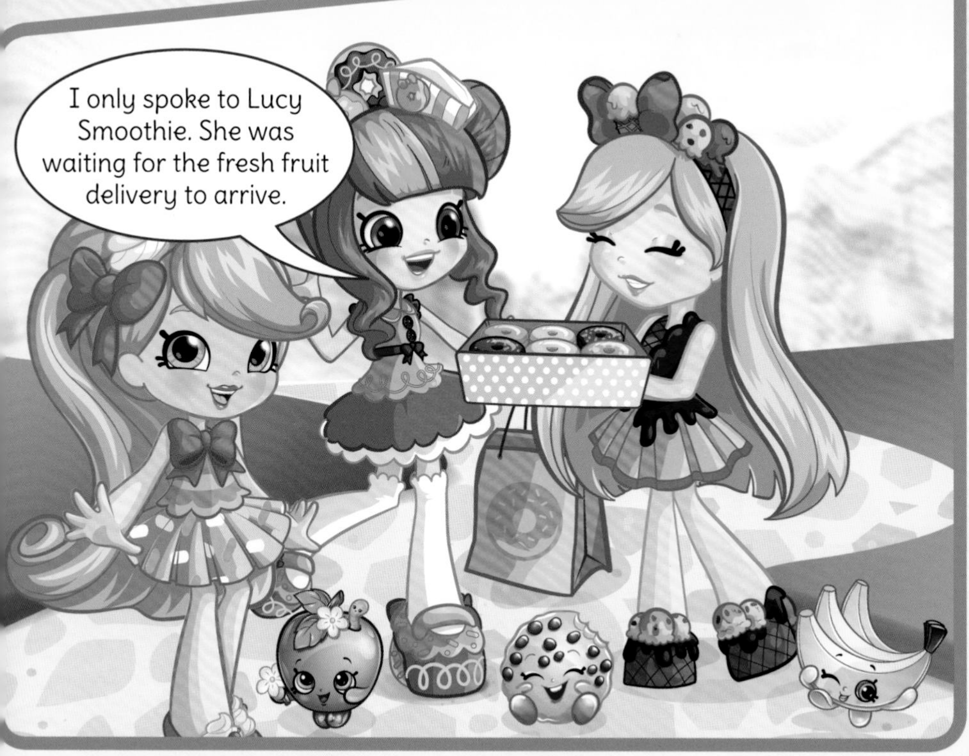
I only spoke to Lucy Smoothie. She was waiting for the fresh fruit delivery to arrive.

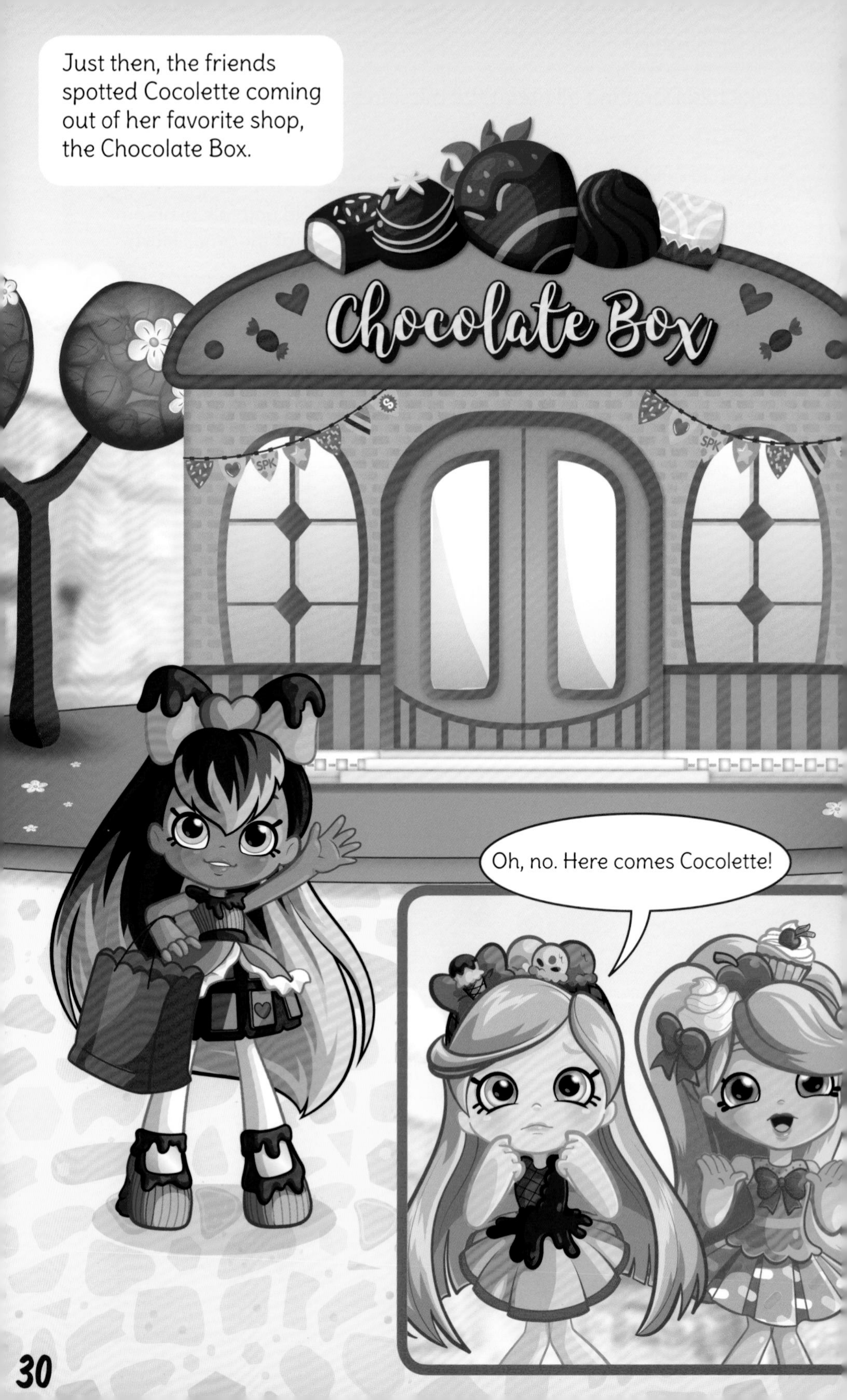
Just then, the friends spotted Cocolette coming out of her favorite shop, the Chocolate Box.
Chocolate Box
SPK
SPK
Oh, no. Here comes Cocolette!

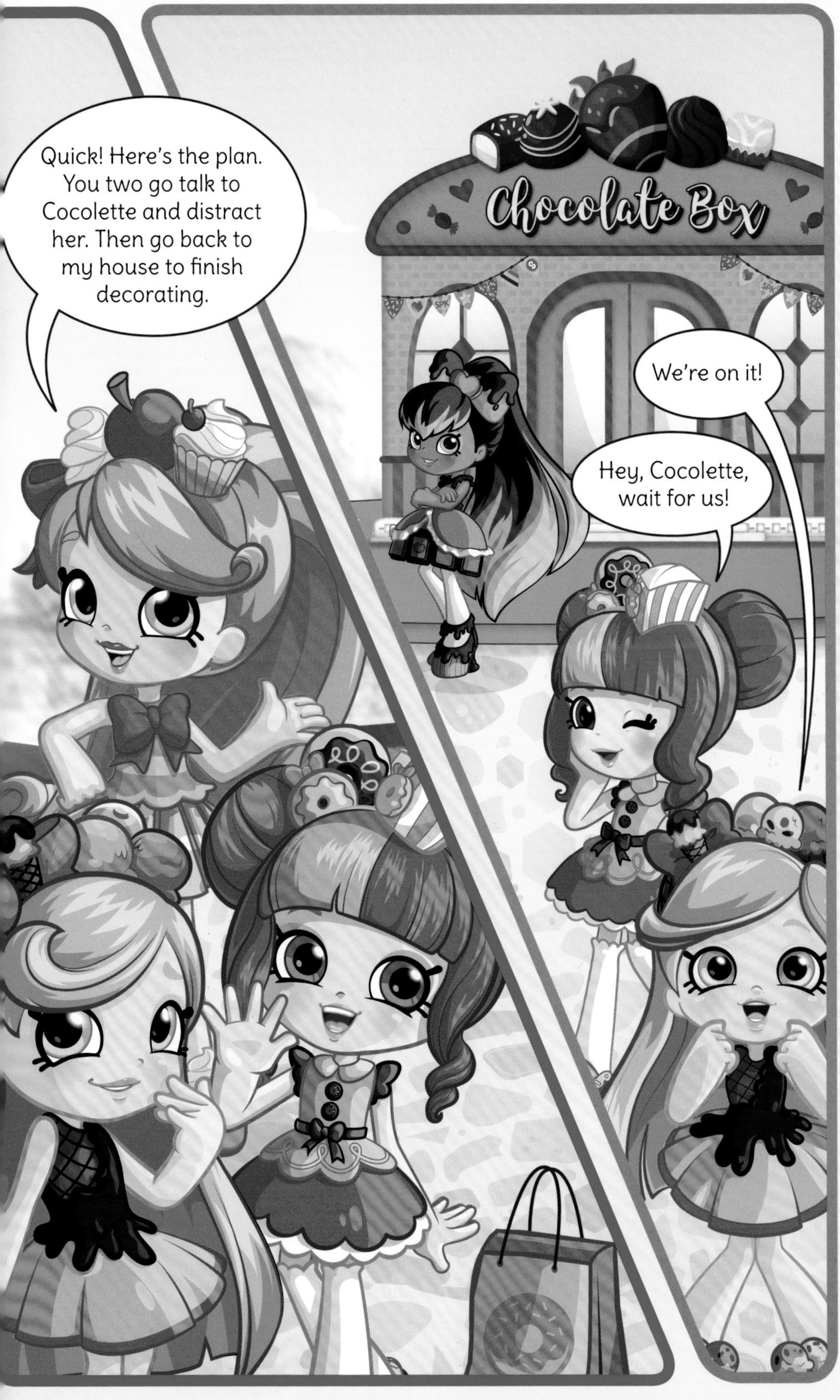
Quick! Here's the plan. You two go talk to Cocolette and distract her. Then go back to my house to finish decorating.
Chocolate Box
We're on it!
Hey, Cocolette, wait for us!

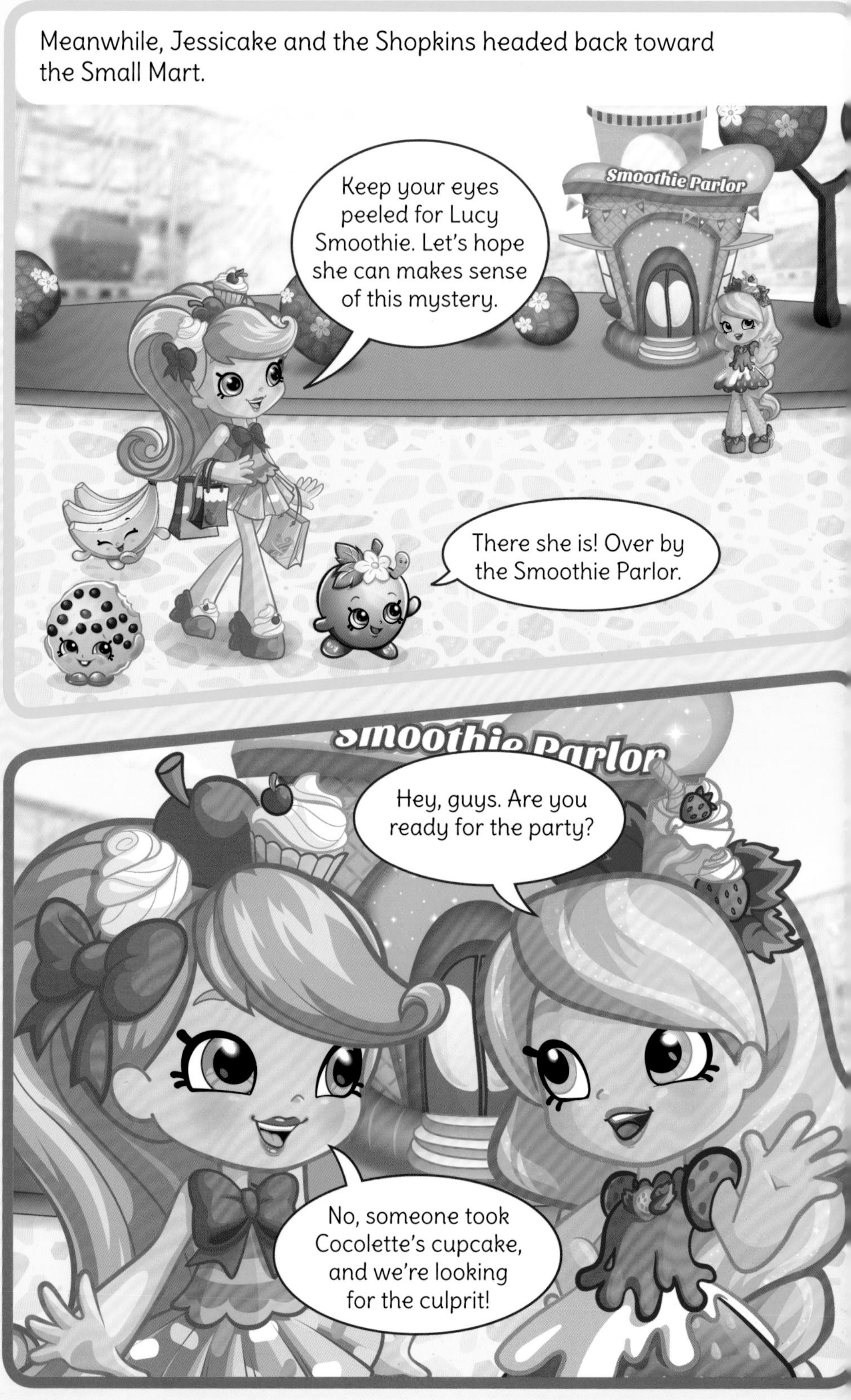
Meanwhile, Jessicake and the Shopkins headed back toward the Small Mart.
Smoothie Parlor
Keep your eyes peeled for Lucy Smoothie. Let's hope she can makes sense of this mystery.
There she is! Over by the Smoothie Parlor.
Hey, guys. Are you ready for the party?
No, someone took Cocolette's cupcake, and we're looking for the culprit!

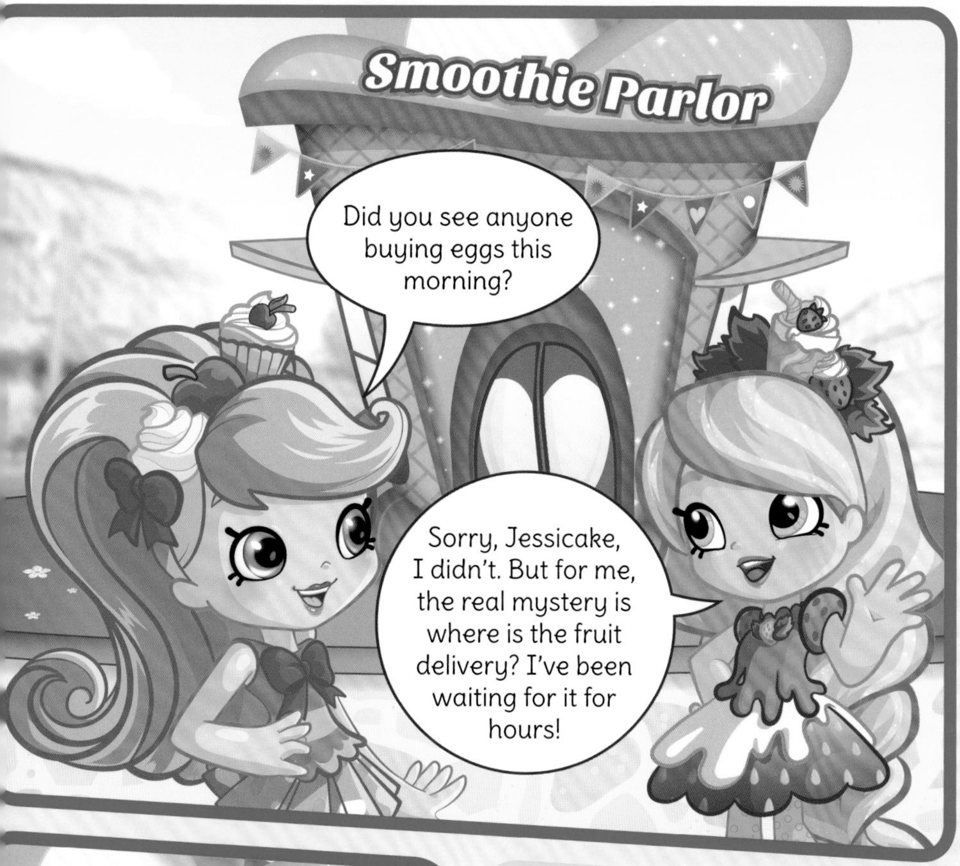
Smoothie Parlor
Did you see anyone buying eggs this morning?
Sorry, Jessicake, I didn't. But for me, the real mystery is where is the fruit delivery? I've been waiting for it for hours!

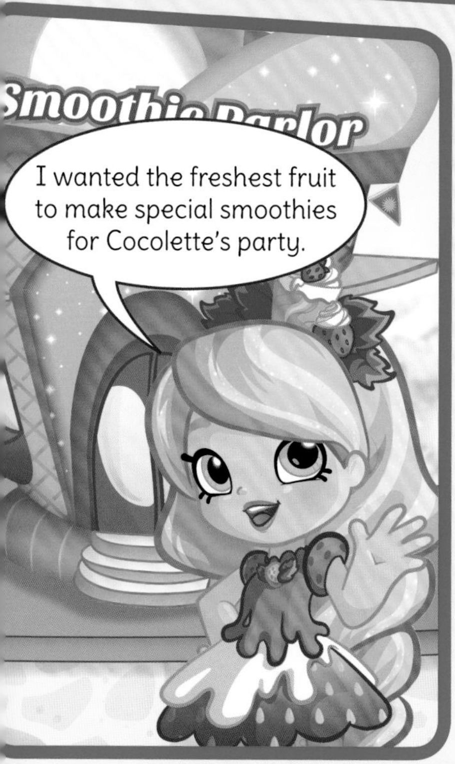
I wanted the freshest fruit to make special smoothies for Cocolette's party.

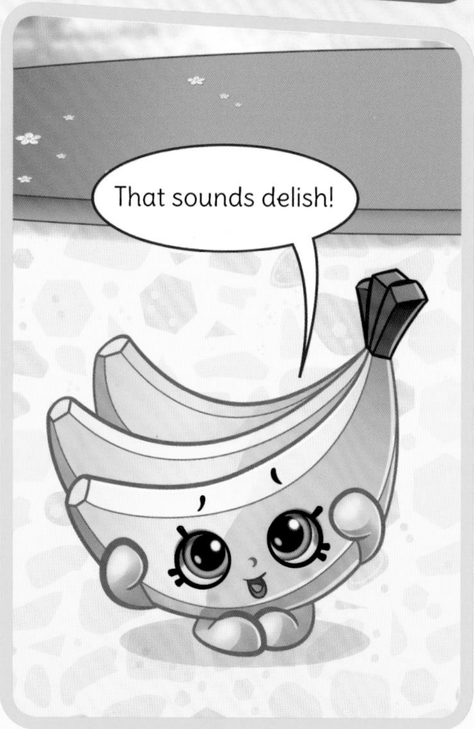
That sounds delish!

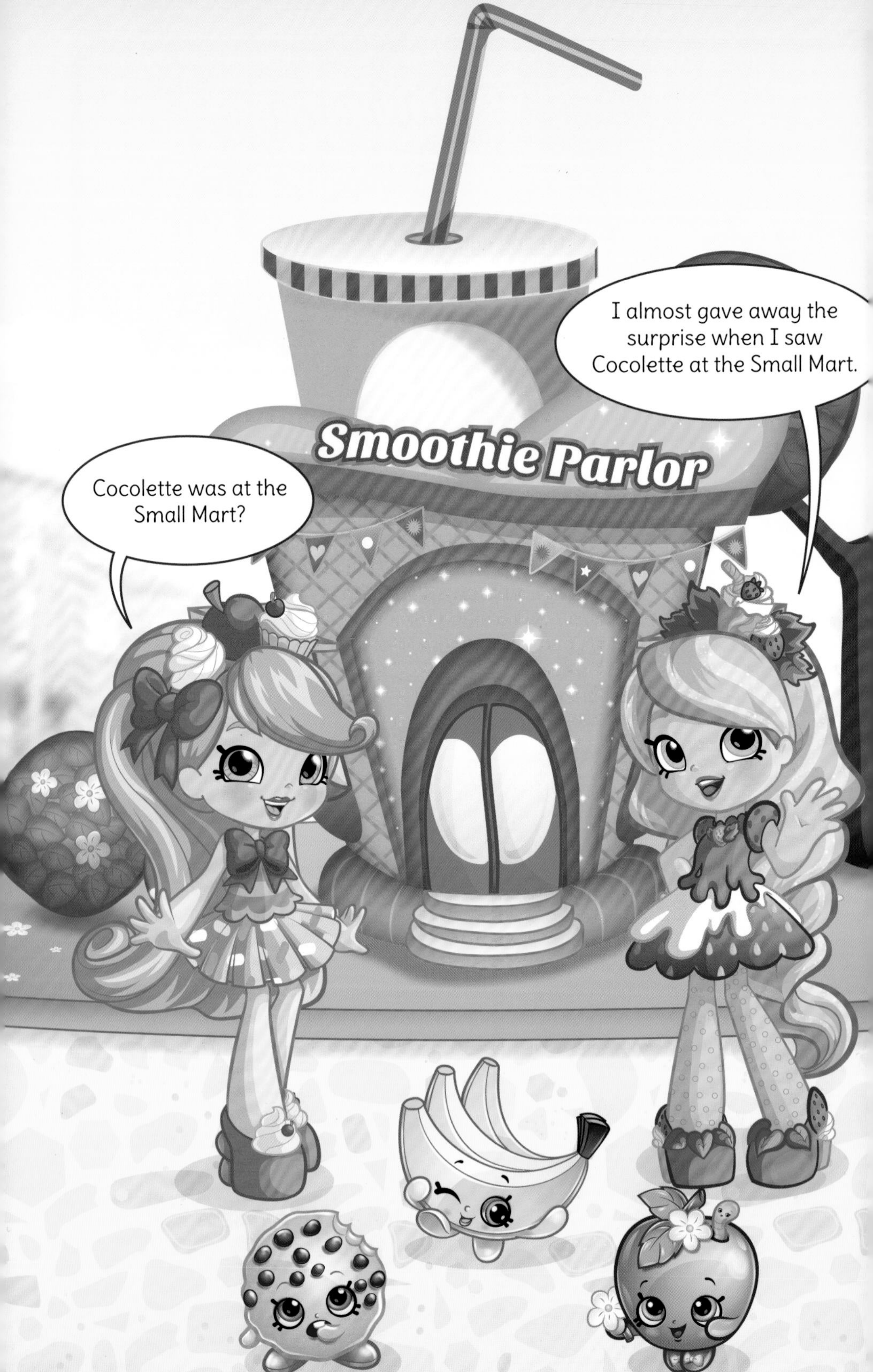
Smoothie Parlor
Cocolette was at the Small Mart?
I almost gave away the surprise when I saw Cocolette at the Small Mart.

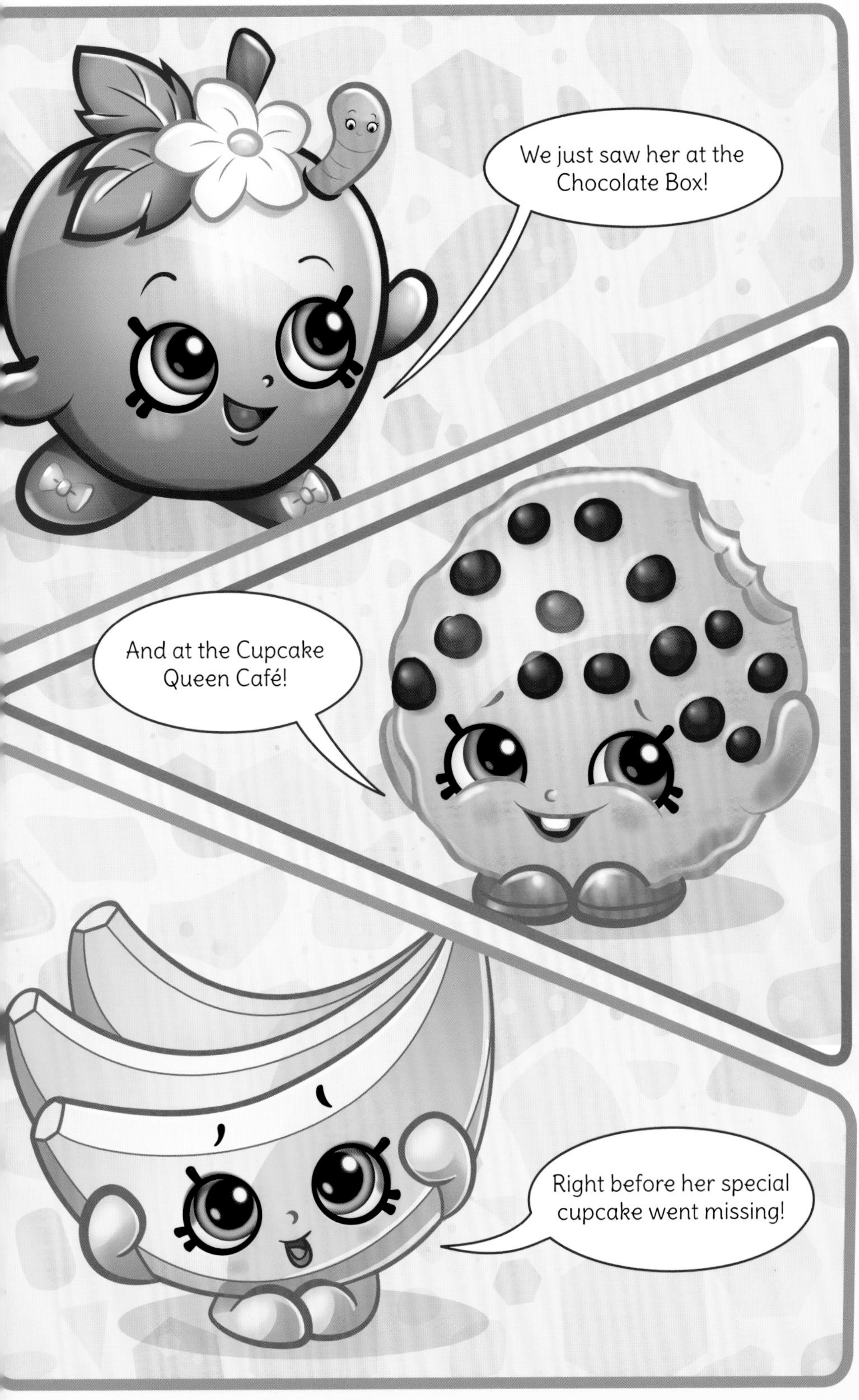
We just saw her at the Chocolate Box!
And at the Cupcake Queen Café!
Right before her special cupcake went missing!

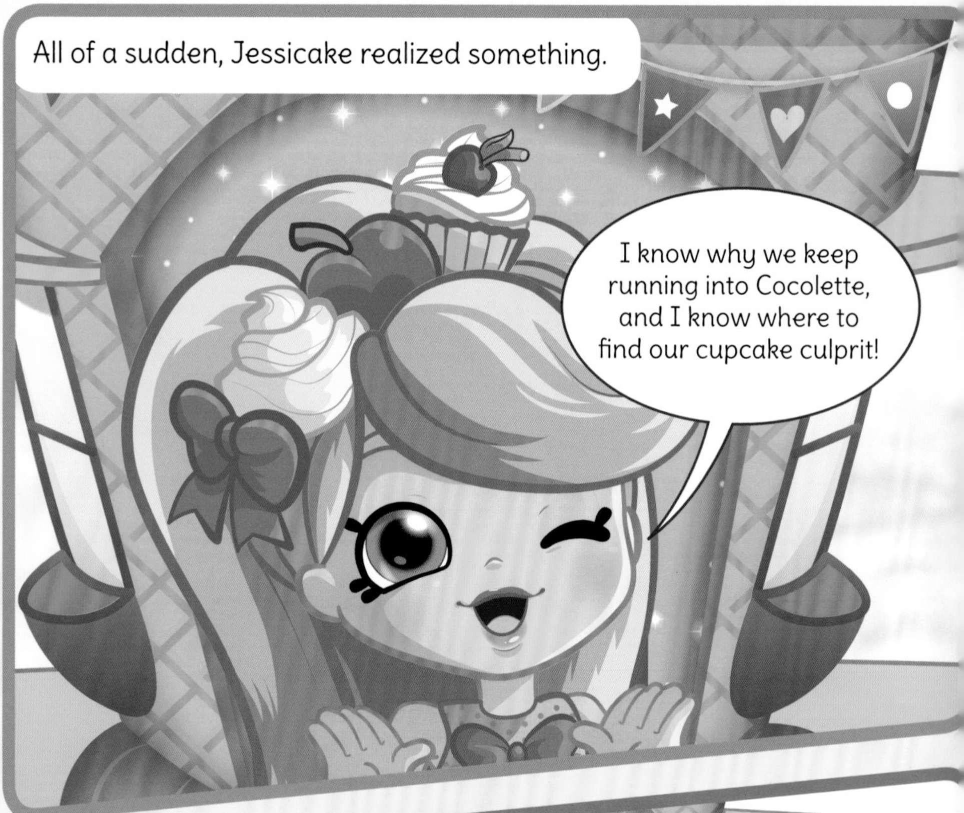
All of a sudden, Jessicake realized something.
I know why we keep running into Cocolette, and I know where to find our cupcake culprit!

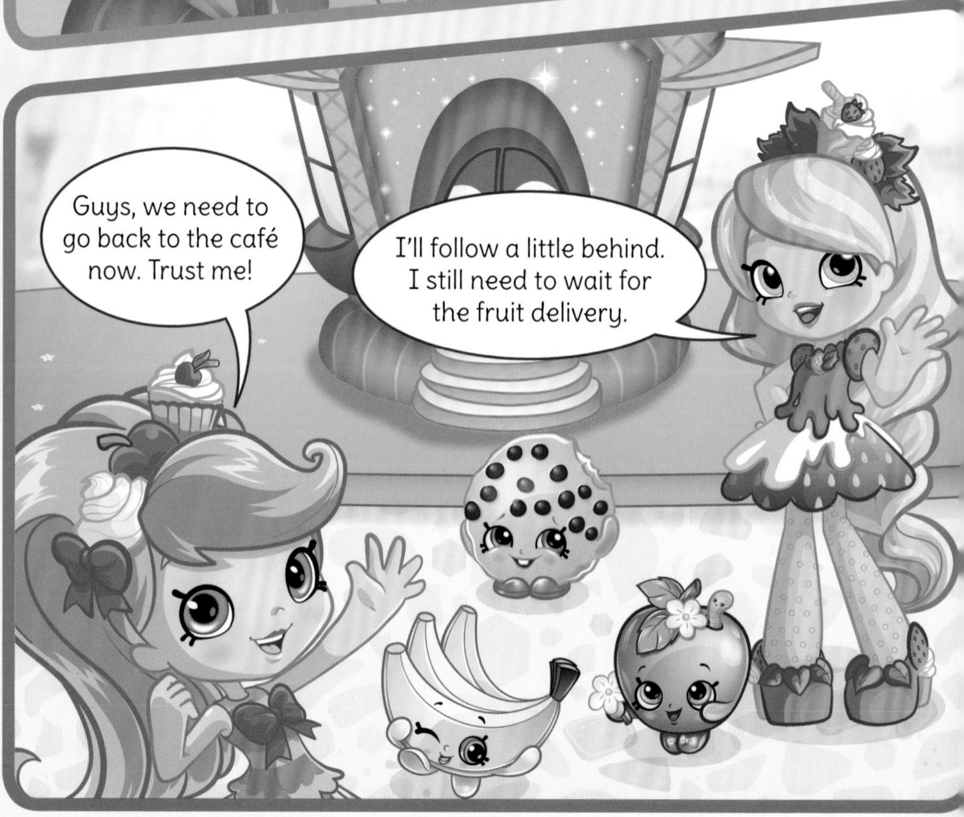
Guys, we need to go back to the café now. Trust me!
I'll follow a little behind. I still need to wait for the fruit delivery.

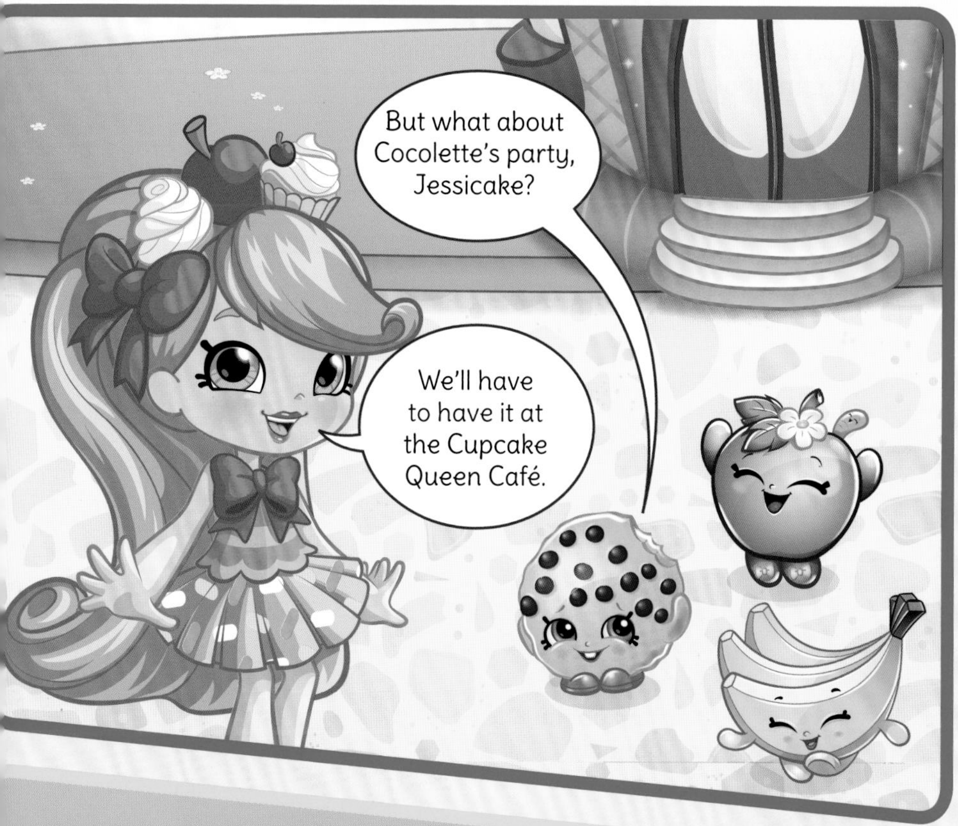
But what about Cocolette's party, Jessicake?
We'll have to have it at the Cupcake Queen Café.

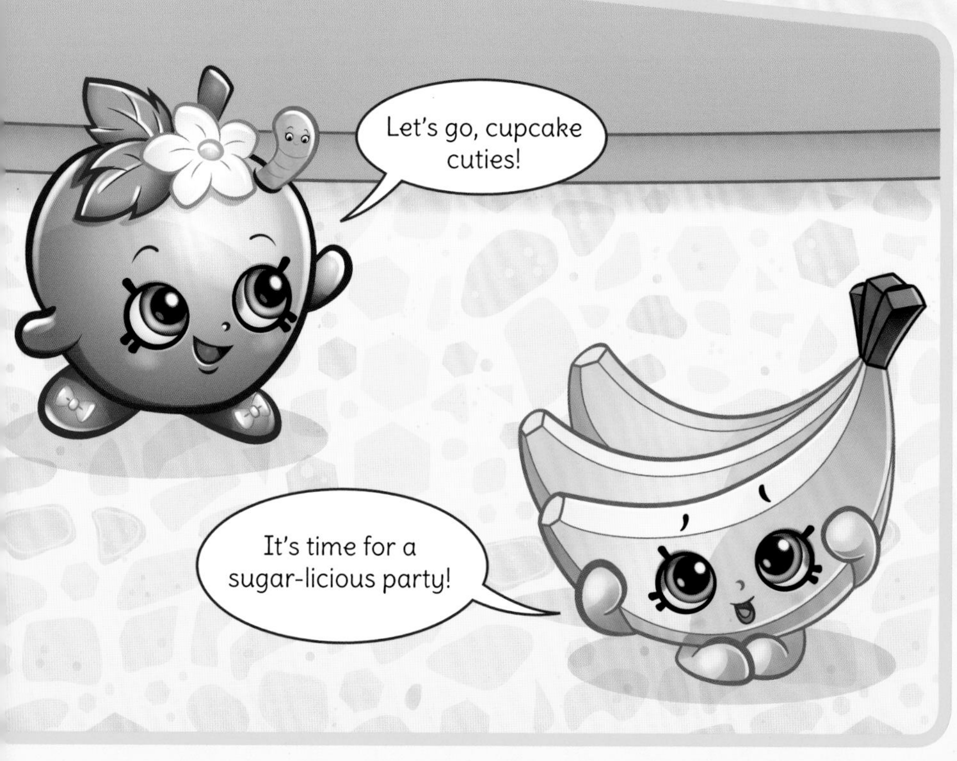
Let's go, cupcake cuties!
It's time for a sugar-licious party!

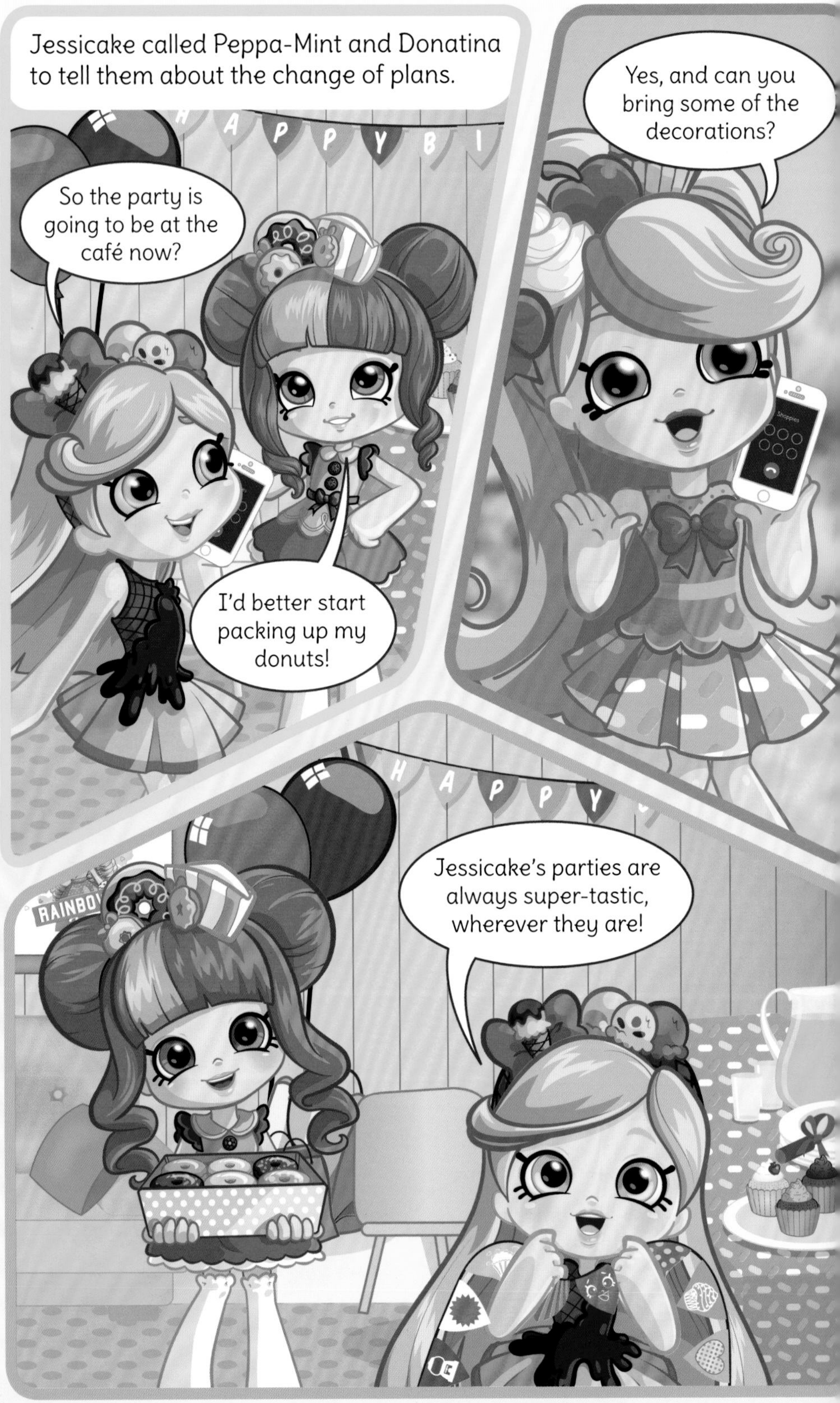
Jessicake called Peppa-Mint and Donatina to tell them about the change of plans.
HAPPY BI
So the party is going to be at the café now?
I'd better start packing up my donuts!
Yes, and can you bring some of the decorations?
HAPPY
RAINBOW
Jessicake's parties are always super-tastic, wherever they are!

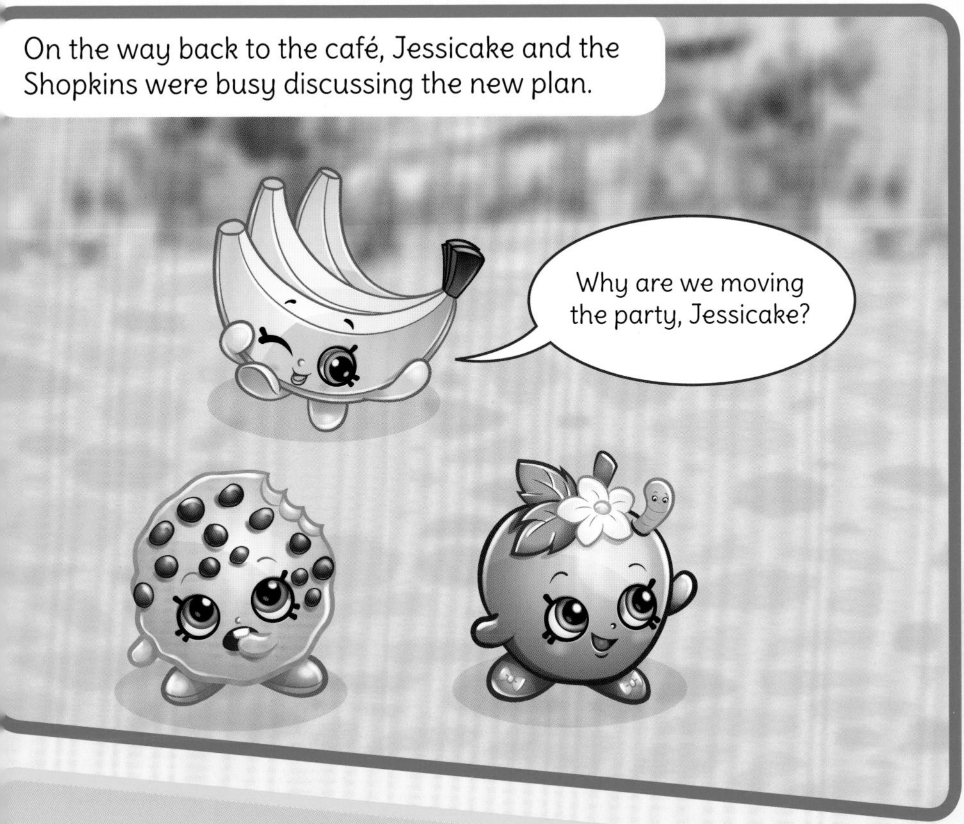
On the way back to the café, Jessicake and the Shopkins were busy discussing the new plan.
Why are we moving the party, Jessicake?

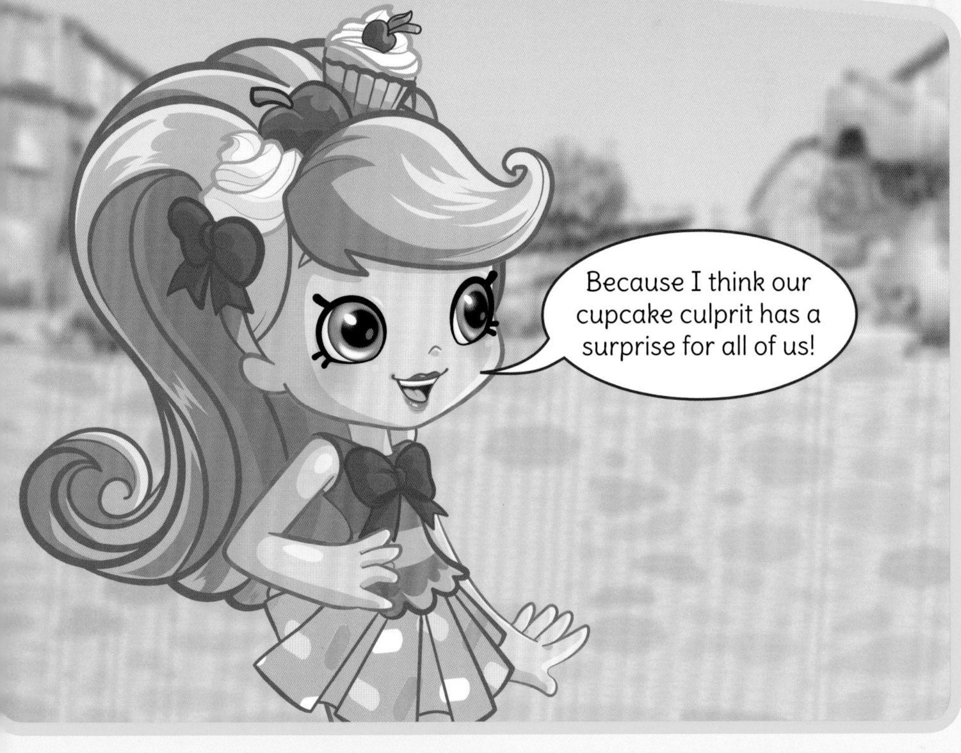
Because I think our cupcake culprit has a surprise for all of us!

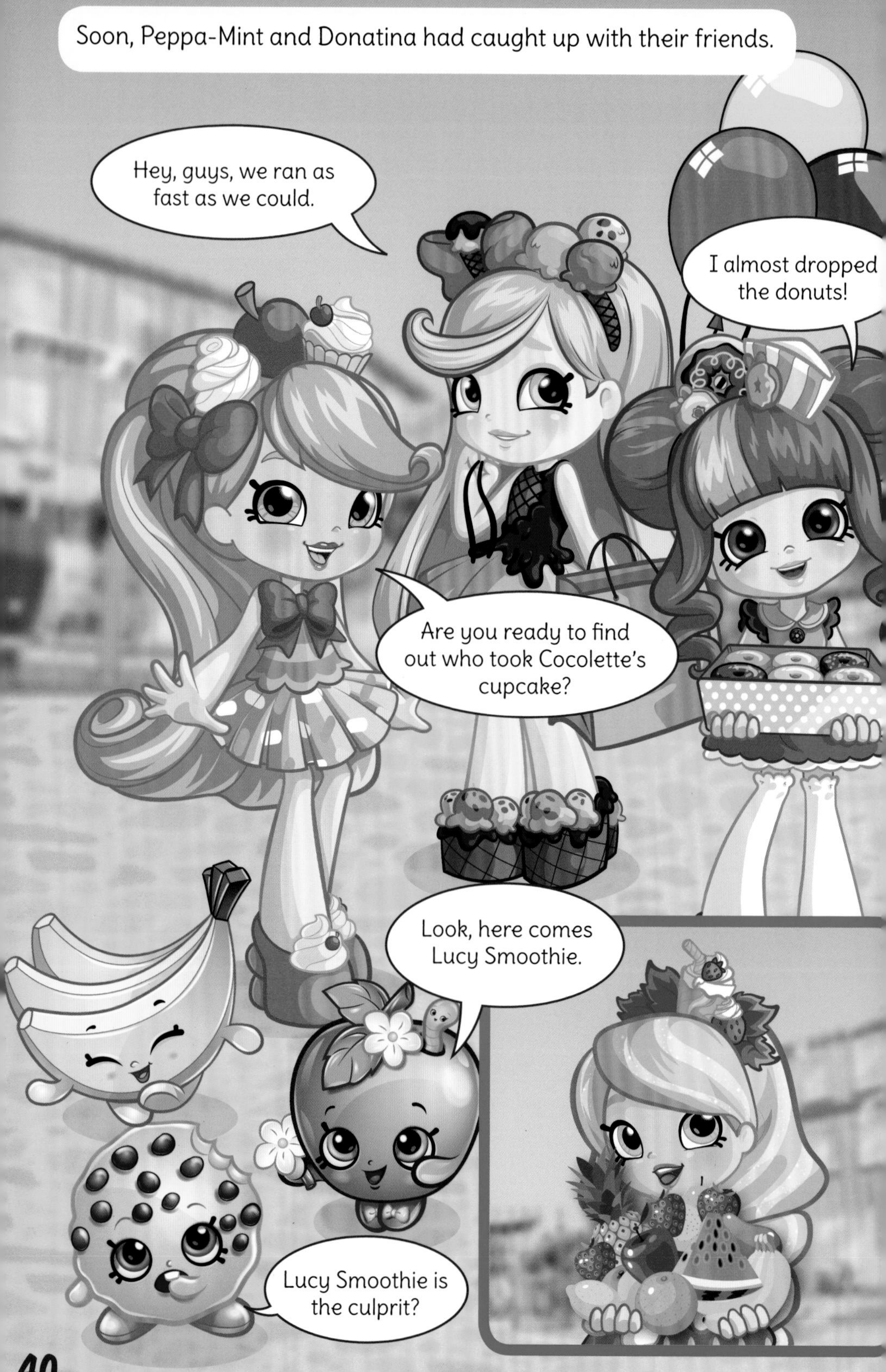
Soon, Peppa-Mint and Donatina had caught up with their friends.
Hey, guys, we ran as fast as we could.
I almost dropped the donuts!
Are you ready to find out who took Cocolette's cupcake?
Look, here comes Lucy Smoothie.
Lucy Smoothie is the culprit?

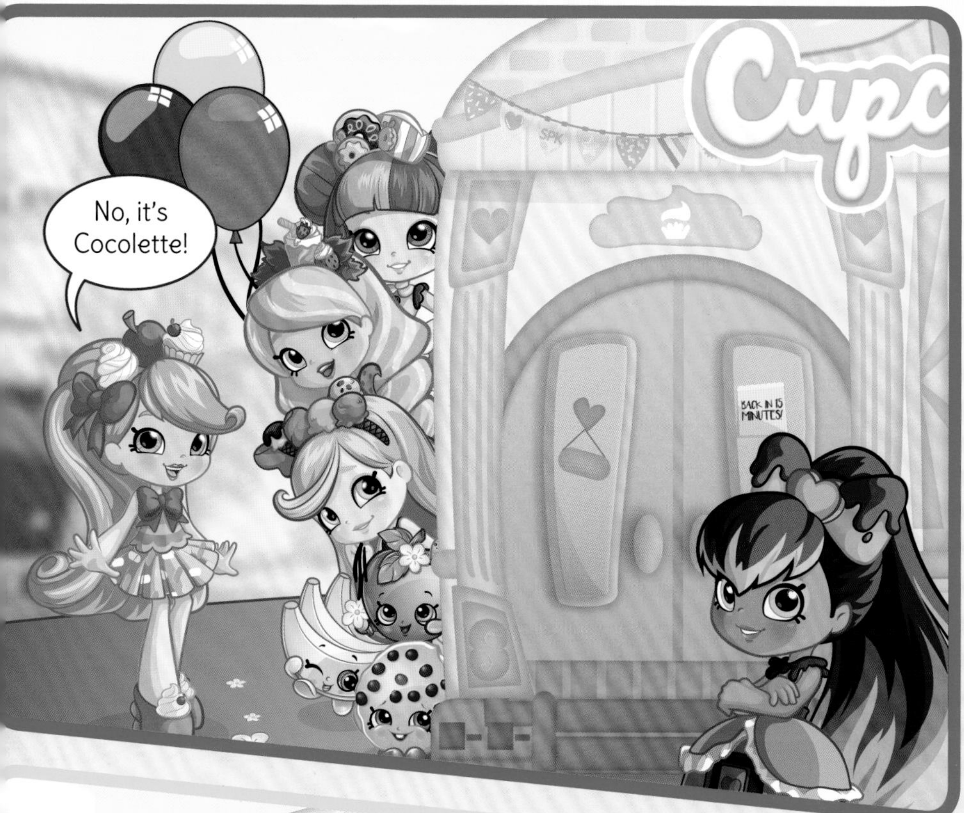
Cupc
No, it's Cocolette!
BACK IN 15 MINUTES!

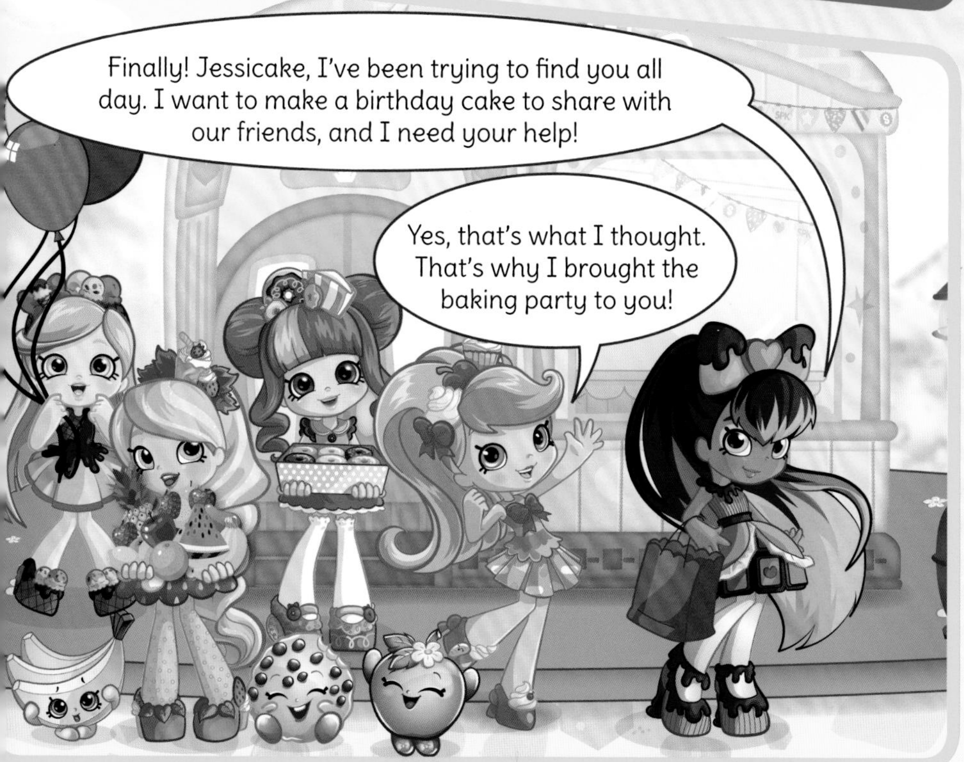
Finally! Jessicake, I've been trying to find you all day. I want to make a birthday cake to share with our friends, and I need your help!
Yes, that's what I thought. That's why I brought the baking party to you!

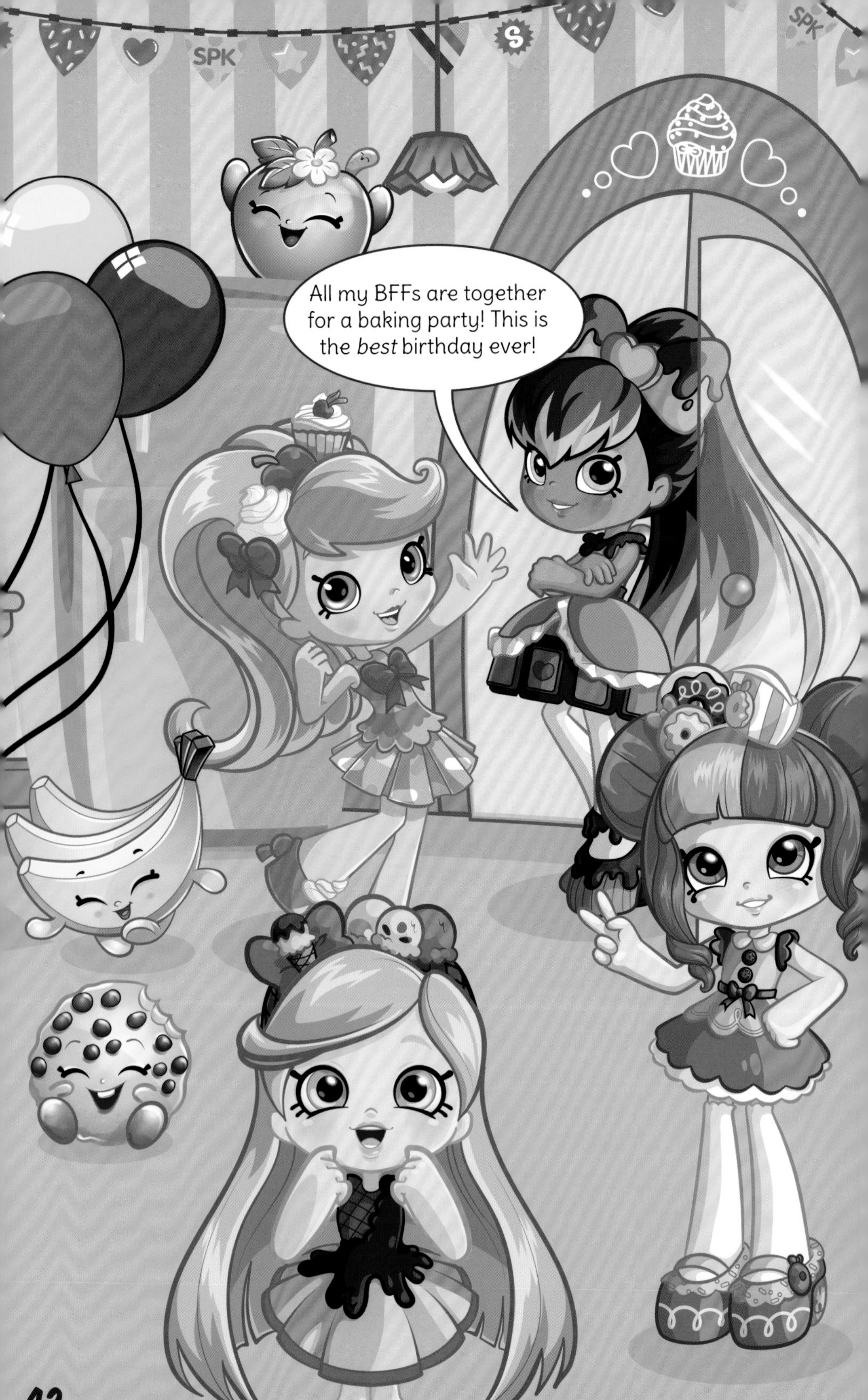
All my BFFs are together for a baking party! This is the *best* birthday ever!

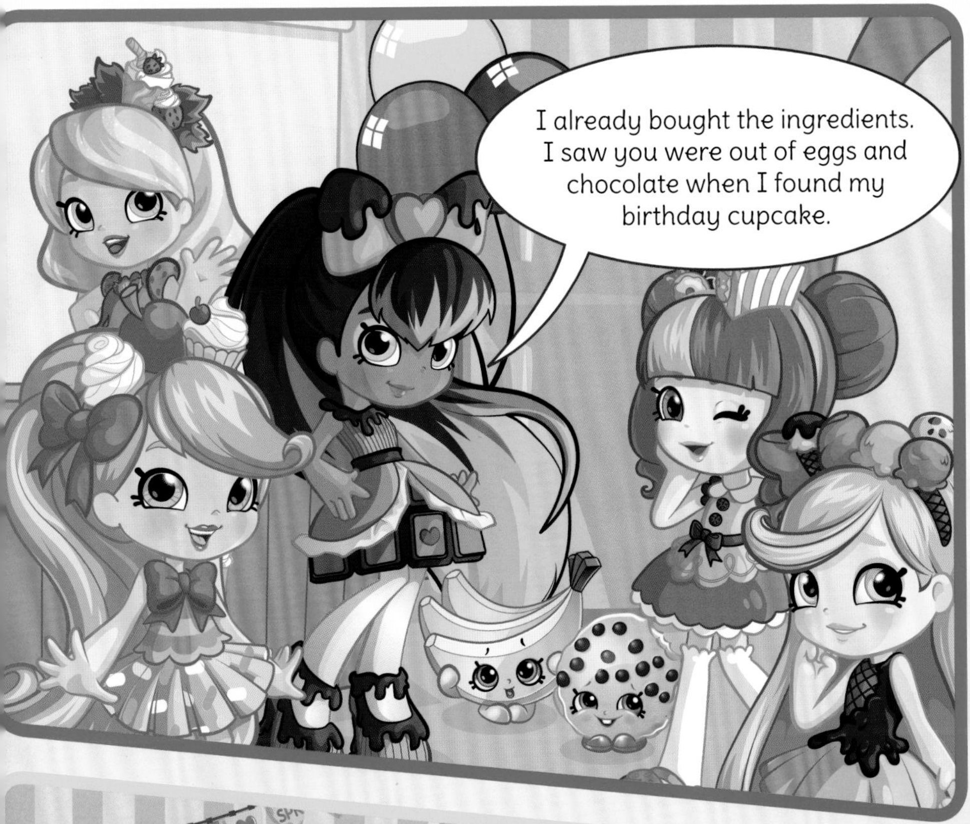
I already bought the ingredients. I saw you were out of eggs and chocolate when I found my birthday cupcake.

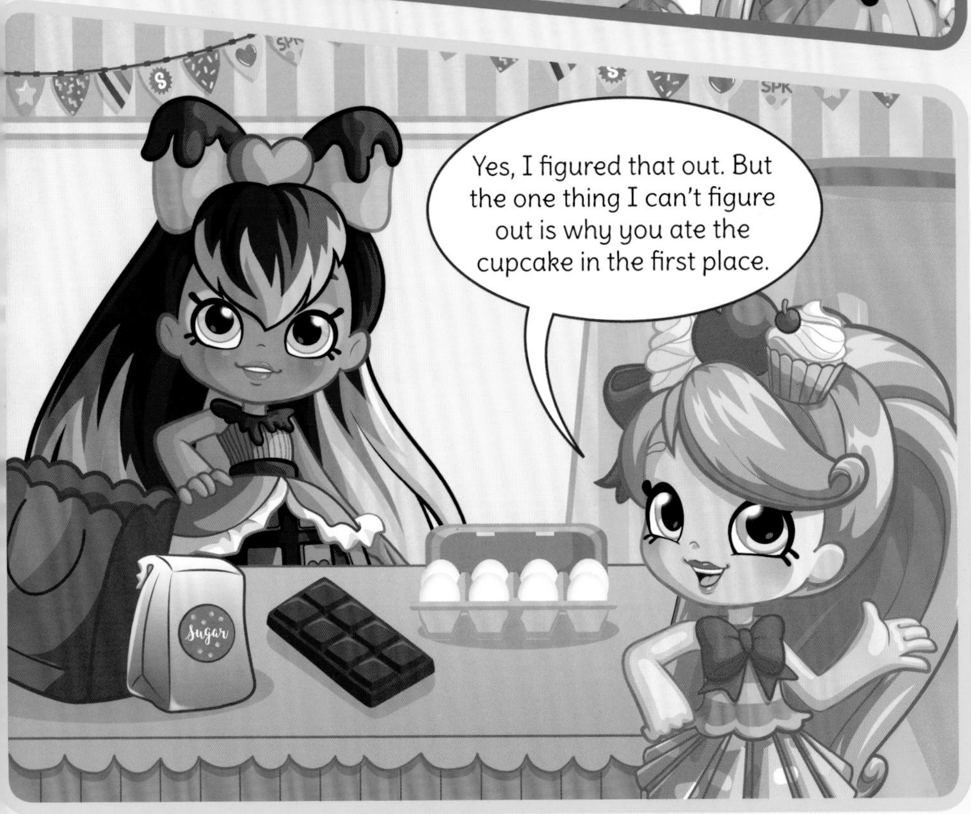
SPK
SPK
Yes, I figured that out. But the one thing I can't figure out is why you ate the cupcake in the first place.
Sugar

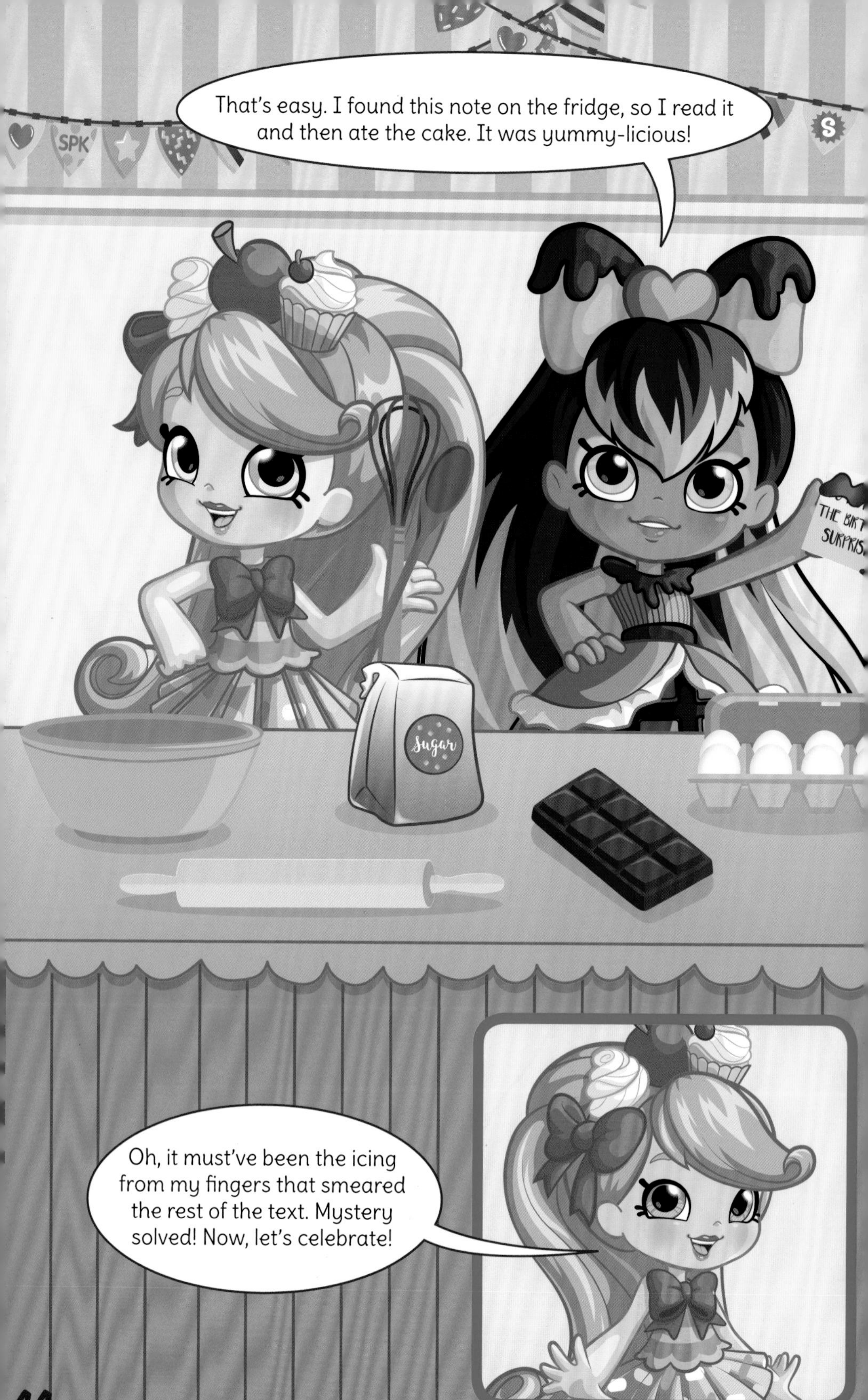

SPK
S
That's easy. I found this note on the fridge, so I read it and then ate the cake. It was yummy-licious!
THE BIRT SURPRIS.
Sugar
Oh, it must've been the icing from my fingers that smeared the rest of the text. Mystery solved! Now, let's celebrate!

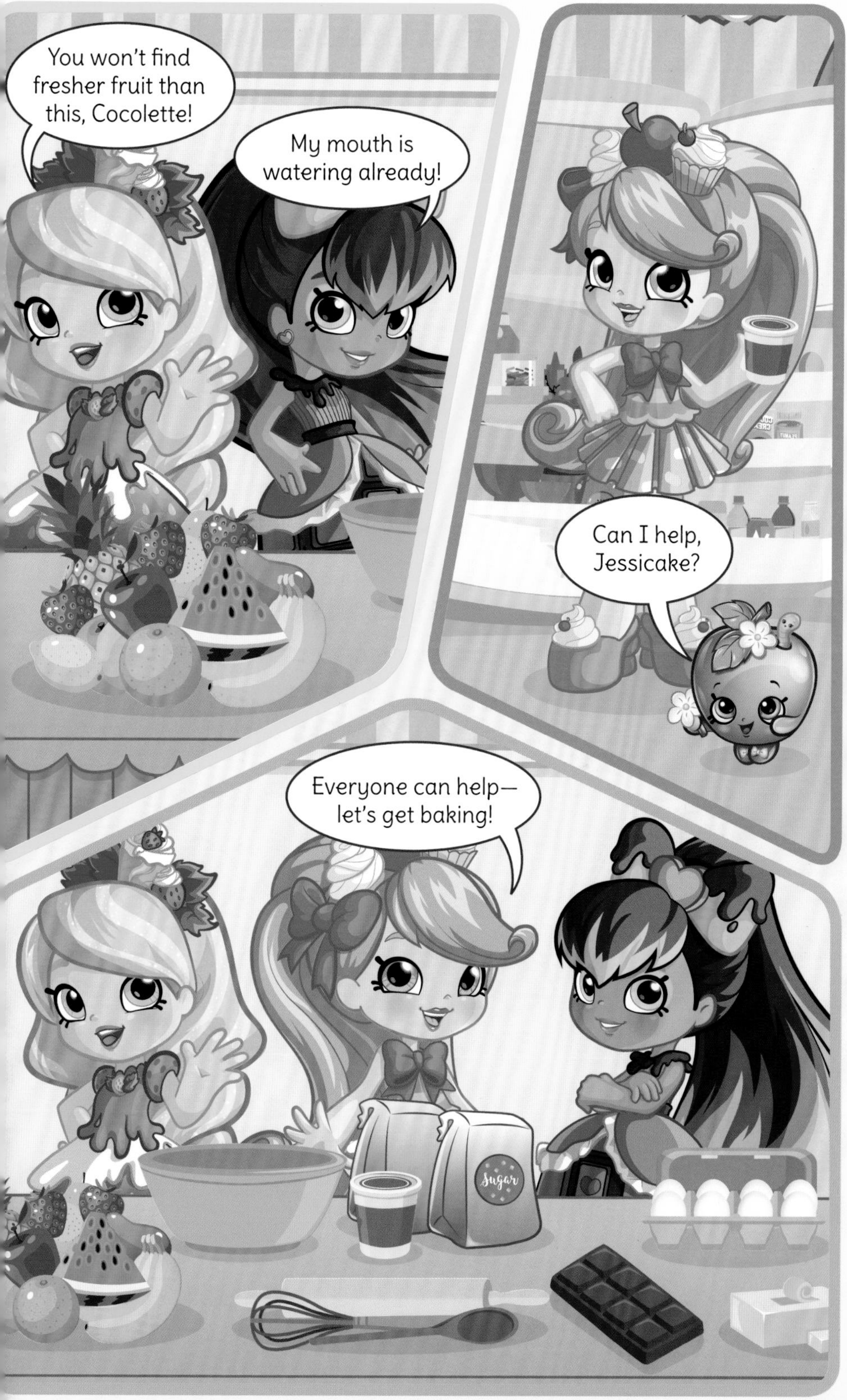
You won't find fresher fruit than this, Cocolette!
My mouth is watering already!
Can I help, Jessicake?
Everyone can help—let's get baking!
Sugar

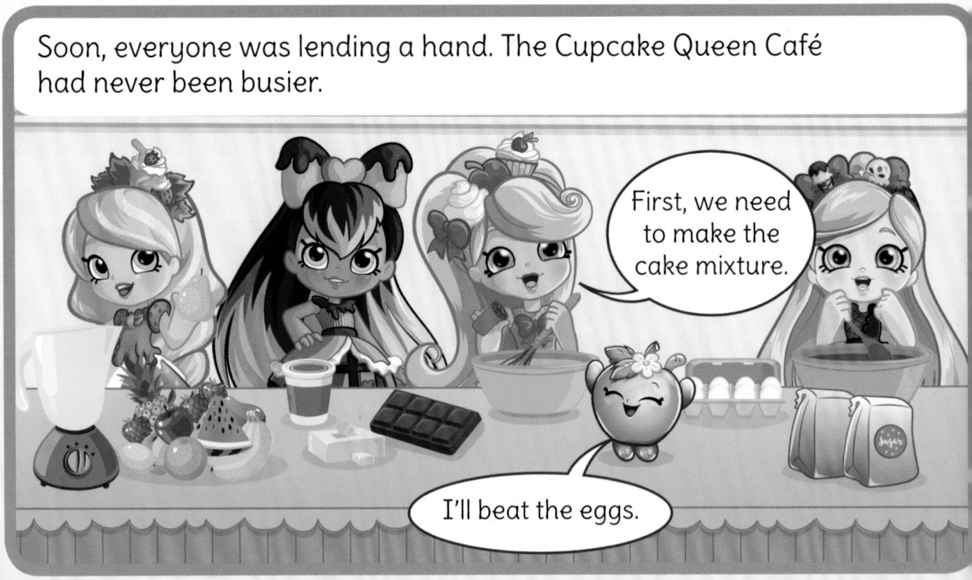
Soon, everyone was lending a hand. The Cupcake Queen Café had never been busier.
First, we need to make the cake mixture.
I'll beat the eggs.

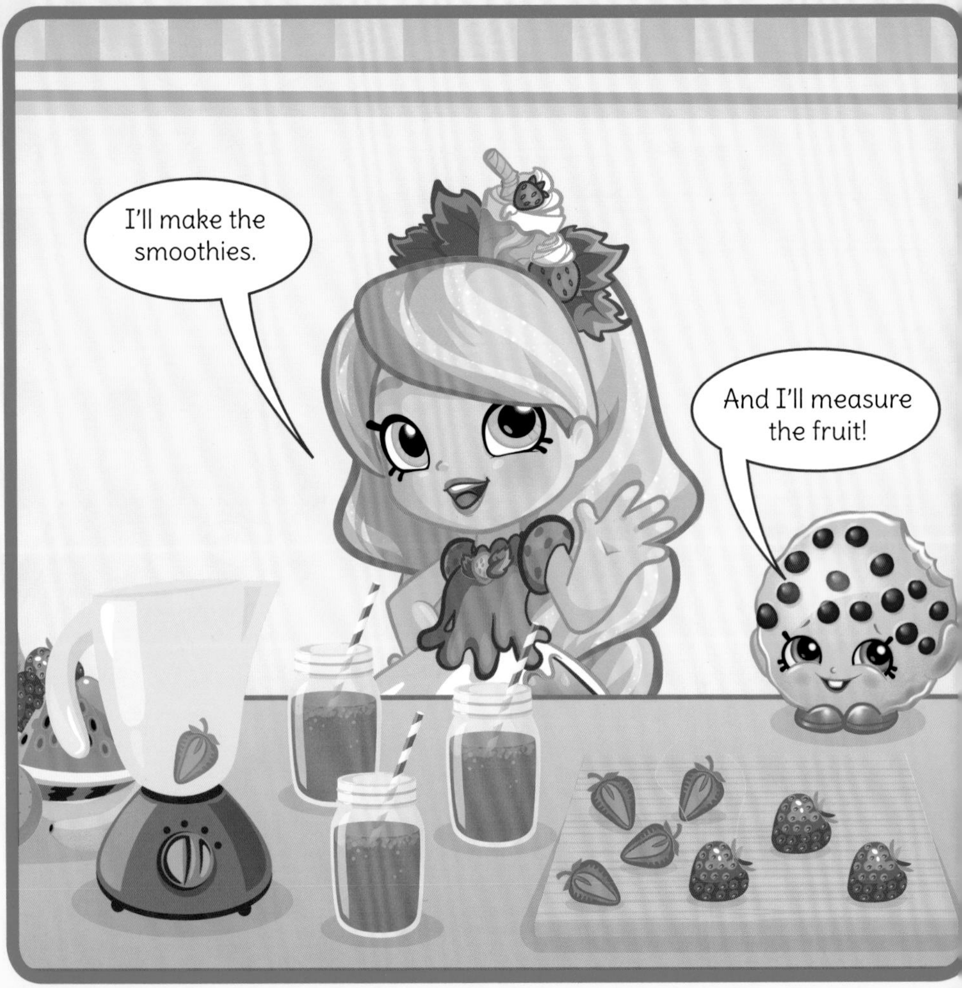
I'll make the smoothies.
And I'll measure the fruit!

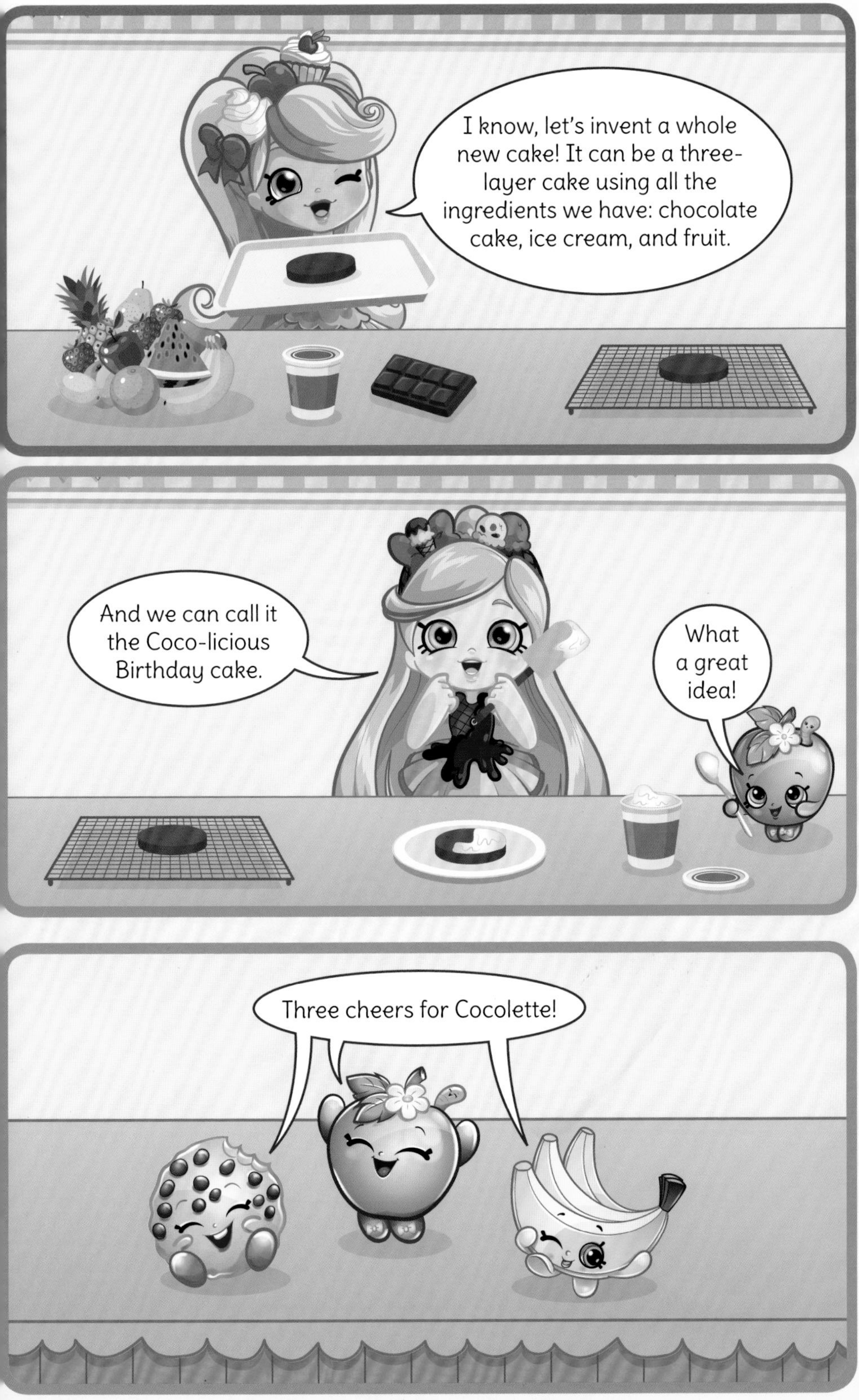

I know, let's invent a whole new cake! It can be a three-layer cake using all the ingredients we have: chocolate cake, ice cream, and fruit.
And we can call it the Coco-licious Birthday cake.
What a great idea!
Three cheers for Cocolette!

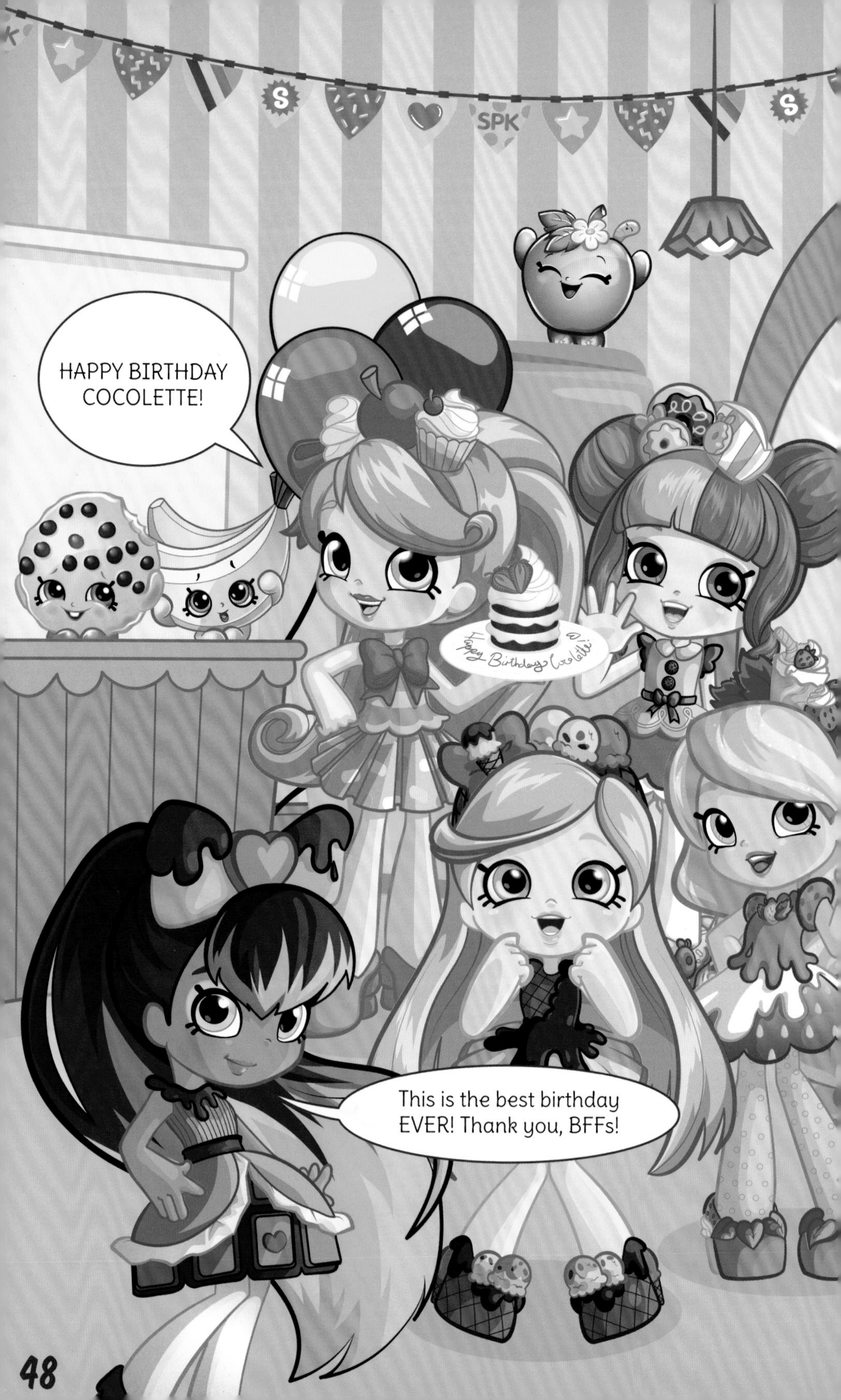

SPK
HAPPY BIRTHDAY COCOLETTE!
Happy Birthday Cocolette!
This is the best birthday EVER! Thank you, BFFs!